Thanks and Acknowledgements

I would like to thank Tiffany Shand of Write Now Creative. She has been a brilliant mentor and editor and I wouldn't have got this far without her.

I would also like to thank Abby Simmons of abbydesignsit on Fiverr for the beautiful artwork she created for my cover. She was a joy to work with.

Another huge thank you to the lovely author Emily Harvale. She is the author of a large number of romantic fiction books and I love them all. Emily has been very kind in offering me lots of valuable advice in looking for an editor and self-publishing.

And finally, a great big thank you to my husband Mark who has supported me all the way in achieving my dream to publish a book.

CHAPTER ONE

Nikki Pembroke drove her white van emblazoned with the name of her dad's business, Pembroke Decorating Services through Honesty, a beautiful village set near hills and lakes. It was a popular tourist destination with an abundance of quaint shops and tea rooms set around the village pond. She was feeling very excited. Her dad, Chris, had tendered for and won a contract to decorate all the buildings at a new writers and artists' retreat. The retreat was owned by her favourite author Paul Archer, a world-renowned crime writer and Nikki was hoping to have the opportunity to meet him and talk about the books she enjoyed so much.

The satnav took her out to the other side of the village and onto a road where the trees which were moving gently in the breeze, provided a lovely green canopy overhead. Just as she was told that she had reached her destination Nikki saw the sign for Burbridge Hall and turned into the long, gravel drive flanked by topiary sculptures of birds and animals. Soon she came to a fork in the road. A sign saying that the hall now a conference centre and hotel, was on the left and that the car park for the Archers Folly contractors was further up on the right. Nikki continued up to the contractors' car park where she saw a man standing next to a golf buggy. She parked nearby and took a couple of deep breaths before exiting her van with a beaming smile. This was going to be the first time she had managed a large-scale decorating project and she didn't want to let her dad down.

She strode confidently towards the man. He was wearing light blue jeans, a Rolling Stones T-shirt that had obviously seen better days and a pair of tan rigger boots. He had a big bushy beard and brown, wild curly hair.

"Mike Dean, I presume." She shook his hand and took in the piercing blue eyes that observed her.

"And you are?"

"Nikki Pembroke, I believe you're expecting me. I'm leading the decorating team."

Mike smiled as he looked at the pretty blonde woman standing in front of him. She was slim with her blonde hair styled in a high ponytail wearing jeans and a T-shirt bearing the same name and logo as the side of her van. Her beautiful green eyes were opened wide unable to disguise how nervous she was feeling.

"Forgive me, Nikki, I was expecting a Nick Pembroke."

7

"It's not the first time people have expected a man to turn up," Nikki said. "My father has often called me Nik. I'm good at my job, so you won't be disappointed, I promise."

"Let's start the grand tour then." Mike motioned her to join him in the golf buggy. "This is the quickest and easiest way to get around the site and we've made a number of buggies available for use by our contractors."

"That's a great idea!"

"So, Archers Folly is of course the brainchild of the author Paul Archer who has always had the dream of opening a centre for writers, artists and creatives. He purchased Burbridge Hall six years ago. It was horribly run down, and the family simply couldn't afford the upkeep anymore."

"A lot of stately homes seem to end up being owned by the National Trust for that very reason."

"Paul bought it and set about turning it into a hotel with attached conference and sports centre for use by the delegates. It took over two years to get all the planning permissions in place and then a further two years to manage the monumental task of gutting it as far as we were able to with listed building constraints as well as putting on a new roof."

"It must have seemed never-ending at the time," said Nikki.

Mike nodded. "It was an uphill struggle, but well worth it. The hotel is stunning, and the conference centre is state of the art. It's fully booked now for the next eighteen months. Once that was completed we could start work on Archer's Folly."

The buggy had reached the end of the service road leading upwards from the contractors' car park and stopped so that Nikki could take in the panoramic view of Archer's Folly. The vista stretched out front of her with a tranquil lake in the distance, and a huge courtyard. This wasn't what she had imagined at all. Mike chuckled. "I had a feeling you wouldn't be expecting something like this."

"You're not wrong there." The paperwork her father had given her only listed the number and dimensions of the buildings that they were going to be working on and the paint colours that would be required. He had put in a tender for the work eighteen months ago and she remembered him telling her that the buildings hadn't been built at that point.

They drove down an orange brick road to the large arched gated entrance into the enormous medieval-style courtyard. In the centre there was a fountain topped by a statue of a cloaked archer.

"This is going to be known as the Artisan Square. There are ten units here with apartments above. They're going to be leased out to people who will be carrying out a variety of different arts and crafts," said Mike.

They walked around. There were three large units on either side of the courtyard and the other four which ran along the far end were smaller. They were all built out of stone. Large arched windows made from toughened glass stretched the full the length of the frontage of the units.

"The idea is that visitors can observe the arts and crafts taking place here. We'll also invite schools to bring their pupils here for visits. There will be an Archers Folly website where all the arts and crafts can be sold, and we'll open to the public maybe one weekend a month." Mike explained.

"Why is it called Archer's Folly?"

"Ah, that will become apparent a little bit later on."

"Will the shops either side of the gate be open all the time too?" asked Nikki. She had noticed them when they had driven up to the courtyard.

Mike shook his head. "We'll just open them when we have visitors. We'll just need the walls in those to be painted white."

Nikki made another note in her book, pleased that Mike knew exactly what he wanted to be done. "Right, got it," she said.

"OK, let me show you inside this unit." Mike pulled a large keyring out of his jeans pocket as he walked towards the door. Nikki followed behind him.

It was a functional open space with flagstone floors. All lighting and electrical points had been installed. The large windows allowed the natural light to flood inside.

"Once we know who is going to take each unit we'll provide all the equipment that they need in their workshops." Mike crossed to the other side of the room.

There was a door out to the back leading to a storeroom, a small kitchen and cloakroom as well as stairs leading to the apartment above. They walked up the smart mahogany stairs. Mike unlocked the door at the top that opened into an open-plan space with rustic oak flooring. Sunlight flooded in from the skylights above.

"The kitchens and bathrooms are being fitted over the next two weeks, so we'll need your guys to jump straight in once they're finished," said Mike as Nikki nodded making more entries in her notebook.

They walked past the area where the kitchen was going to be installed and towards the bedrooms. The master bedroom was large with its own ensuite. The other two bedrooms each had a door leading into what would be the shared bathroom.

They left the unit and walked back towards the buggy. As they started to drive off, Mike pointed over to a large concrete base just a short distance away from the courtyard.

"In the next couple of months an American diner is going to be built there. This will be open for all staff members from both the folly and the conference centre as well as our visitors. You'll see as we continue our tour that anything goes here at the folly. So, you'll learn not to be too surprised to see a 1950's diner beside a medieval courtyard."

They set off again and drove across an orange brick bridge over a stream and continued along the road through a large, colourful garden filled with wildflowers. Nikki loved the fragrant aromas filling the air. They soon arrived at a small close where a few crooked, whimsical cottages stood, reminiscent of those in the fairy tales Nikki had read when she was a little girl.

She hopped out of the buggy, keen to get a closer look. "These are delightful! Are they very old?"

Mike chuckled. "No, they're all newly built. Your job will be to paint them in different pastel colours."

There were also two bungalows with wheelchair access. Everything had been thought of. They went inside the first cottage. The front door opened straight into a sitting room with a wood-burning stove set in a small, bricked fireplace. Another door led into a kitchen diner with bi-fold doors which opened out to a small courtyard garden. Upstairs there was a bedroom and a bathroom. Everything was light and airy, a perfect workspace.

"Writers and artists will be able to rent these cottages on short term leases to give them a pleasant, relaxing base to write and draw," said Mike. "Paul is very keen to provide opportunities for people to develop their craft."

Nikki nodded. Paul Archer was a phenomenally successful crime novelist and several of his books had been made into blockbuster movies with A list casts making millions of pounds worldwide. She could understand why he would want to build a retreat like this. It would allow writers to kick back and concentrate on their work while having a break from the real world.

As they moved back outside Nikki looked across at the garden with bees buzzing and settling on the fragrant flowers. She turned to Mike.

"You should hire a beekeeper and make Archer's Folly honey," she said. Nikki's mind was always buzzing with creativity and the honey idea had just come to her in a flash.

Mike stared intensely at her for a moment and then smiled. His blue eyes and dimples made Nikki's heart thump like crazy.

Calm down, Nikki, stay professional. But he is rather gorgeous. She snapped herself out of her thoughts realising that Mike was responding to her suggestion.

"That's an excellent idea! I'm surprised nobody has thought of that before."

"Always happy to help!" She grinned back at him.

They returned to the buggy, and, after a couple of minutes, they arrived at a large Tudor building. It was painted white with black beams forming diamond-shaped patterns. The windows were small and rectangular.

"This will be the retreat for the writers' residential courses, and unsurprisingly we wanted to channel William Shakespeare. It's not original, it's brand spanking new, but we're pleased with it." Mike beamed with pride.

"This is fantastic," replied Nikki, dumbstruck with all the imagination that had gone into the entire site.

"There will be two large, state of the art classrooms downstairs. The rooms for the residential guests are upstairs," Mike explained as they walked in.

"We're certainly going to be very busy getting these ready for you." The rooms downstairs were empty shells just waiting for her team to decorate. They headed upstairs to look at the guest rooms. Mike opened the door to the first one. It was a good size and the ensuite had already been fitted with a smart shower.

"How many people will be working with you here?"

"There'll be eight guys turning up tomorrow. I'll split them into two groups to work on the cottages and this building while we're waiting for the courtyard apartments to be ready for us."

Mike nodded. "Sounds good to me."

After the tour of the building, they left and walked back to the buggy. Another orange brick road lay ahead.

"The yellow brick road idea had already been taken!" joked Mike and they both laughed. Nikki looked sideways at him, those lovely dimples in his cheeks had reappeared as he chuckled away, and something fluttered in her stomach.

Stop it! This is my boss for the next few months.

Mike stopped the buggy once again, and this time Nikki gasped. They had reached the lake she had seen earlier. It had an island in the centre housing what appeared to be an ancient Greek temple with white marble pillars which glistened in the sunlight. Wind chimes tinkled in the gentle breeze. The lake was filled with Koi carp and beautiful lily pads floated on top of the water. White benches were set at intervals around the outside. It was very calming and spiritual.

"So, this is the Folly." Mike swept his hand majestically in front of them. Now the name made sense to Nikki. Follies were buildings that served no purpose and had been built just for the fun of it by wealthy landowners since the sixteenth century

Mike looked at Nikki with concern, she had gone very quiet, "Nikki are you OK?" he asked.

Tears trickled down her cheeks. "I'm sorry for getting emotional. This is so beautiful and peaceful. You see, my father has osteoarthritis, and he's in a lot of pain nowadays which is why I've taken over the decorating. He can answer the phone for the business, but he's getting progressively worse. I worry about him being stuck indoors all the time. Wouldn't it be wonderful if there was somewhere like this for older and housebound people to visit for some respite? They would never tire of having a view like this in such a relaxing environment."

Mike's gorgeous blue eyes looked compassionately into hers and she was sure he could hear her heart pounding away. "You're right. So many people could benefit from living here." he said. "In the meantime, please feel free to bring your father over to enjoy the tranquillity."

Nikki wiped her eyes with a tissue. "Thank you, I'm sure Dad would love it here. It would also give him the opportunity to inspect our work."

"I have one more building to show you," said Mike as they returned to the buggy once again.

They drove alongside an orchard where fragrant cherry and apple blossom trees were in full bloom. They turned a corner and Nikki's mouth opened in surprise.

"I can't believe this!" I'm lost for words!" The buggy came to a halt. She jumped out and forgetting about Mike for a minute she walked briskly over to the scene in front of her, keen to take it all in. There, standing in the middle of the English countryside was a scaled-down version of a Bavarian castle built from red varnished bricks. A red and white chequered pathway swept up to the large red front door. There was a clock tower to one side and two viewing turrets to the other. Mike quickly caught up with Nikki and watched with a smile on his face as she shook her head taking everything in. They walked up the grand pathway and once again Mike produced his key ring ready to unlock the grand door. They entered a large square hallway with a magnificent sweeping staircase. The plastered walls were crying out to be painted and Nikki couldn't wait to get to work on them.

"This has been created for artists to both work and teach in," explained Mike.

"We actually got the planning permission to build this before they approved the changes to Burbridge Hall. As you saw just now in the writer's building there is also good accommodation upstairs for attendees of our residential courses. We want to invite artists, sculptors, and potters to make use of this space. Paul has also invited local schools to make use of our facilities for free. It was the education slant that won the planning department over."

Despite the frontage of the building, the rooms were very modern with good lighting. Nikki was an artist herself and had been an art teacher before she had given her job up to help her dad with his business. She would have loved to have taught in a place like this and she envied the people who would be working here.

"Come and look out the back," said Mike, rubbing his hands together in anticipation.

They walked through a large double door leading outside and once again Nikki was staggered. There were several statues and sculptures set in the middle of a large, beautifully manicured lawn. An enormous white marble head which looked like it had fallen from a statue of a Greek god was lying on its side. A slender metallic hand complete with coloured rings which glistened in the sunlight reached out from the ground and towered above Nikki and Mike. Statues of animals were displayed along with sculptures that left you guessing at what they could possibly be. Nikki walked up to a wooden carved statue of a man at the end of the garden and snorted with laughter.

"Is that.….Simon Cowell?" She laughed.

Mike laughed along with her. "Um, yes it is." He enjoyed Nikki's reaction to the art castle. "We ran a competition a year ago for interesting art to be displayed in the garden and this was one of the entries. It's so beautifully carved and just like you, everybody can see the fun in it. I love it."

"It's absolutely brilliant!" said Nikki, agreeing with him wholeheartedly stopping from time to time to run her hand along the sculptures and statues enjoying the textures of the materials that had been used.

They returned to the front of the castle. "What an amazing vision Paul has had," said Nikki. "His books are so cleverly written with the unexpected plot twists; I can see how his imagination came up with Archers Folly."

"Have you read many of Paul's books?" Mike locked the door to the castle.

"Have I!" exclaimed Nikki. "I own them all! He's the most brilliant writer, my absolute favourite author. I downloaded and read his newest book just after midnight."

"And what did you think of it?" Mike waited for her to answer.

Nikki pulled a face. "Honestly, I was a bit disappointed. Normally it's impossible to guess who the villain is. This time, I worked out that it was Mr Worthington by chapter three and the expected plot twist never happened." She remembered the anticipation the night before as she had waited for her pre-ordered book to appear on her Kindle, then the feeling of being let down by the flimsy storyline.

Mike's whole demeanour changed at this point. He walked briskly to the buggy and Nikki almost had to jog to keep up with him. Without another word, they drove down to where a couple with a little boy sleeping in his pushchair and a little girl skipping around were waiting.

Mike got out of the buggy and waved Nikki forward. "Nikki, let me introduce you to Mike Dean and his wife Cleo," he said without emotion.

Nikki's mouth opened in surprise. "But you told me that your name was Mike," she replied as she shoved her hands in her pockets. The happy expression she had worn on her face throughout the tour was replaced by a look of bewilderment and she fiercely blinked back the tears that were threatening to fall.

He crossed his arms and scowled. "No, if you remember you introduced yourself by saying "Mike Dean, I presume."

"Well, you could have corrected me." Nikki put her hands on her hips and took a couple of steps towards him. "I was so nervous about our meeting, and I was trying to make a good impression. Dad told me that I was being met by Mike Dean. What's your name, then?"

"Surely you would have recognised Paul Archer your favourite author?" He frowned at her.

Nikki flushed bright red. "I wouldn't even recognise my own brother with that scruffy hair and bushy beard!" she answered back at once regretting it.

Without saying another word, Paul Archer turned on his heel and stomped away.

CHAPTER TWO

Nikki buried her face in her hands. "What have I just done?"

Cleo spoke first, putting a friendly arm around her shoulder, "Come back home with us for a while, a nice cup of tea and a chat will help."

Nikki looked up. Cleo was a tall, beautiful black woman with gorgeous, braided hair. She was wearing dark skinny jeans with an open cerise shirt over a white tank top and looked kind and friendly. The real Mike was well built with designer stubble and a neat haircut. He was wearing jeans with a red checked plaid shirt with the sleeves rolled up. He had watched in confusion as Paul had stormed off wondering why he hadn't told Nikki the truth about who he was.

"Don't worry about Paul, something has obviously rattled his cage. His mood swings are legendary but normally quite short-lived." He smiled.

Nikki nervously fiddled with the scrunchy keeping her ponytail in place. "I rattled his cage. We had a brilliant tour of the whole project and then he asked me what I thought of Paul's latest book as I had just declared myself to be a super fan. I told him it was disappointing and well, you know the rest."

"Ouch!" agreed Mike. "Well, let's get back to the house, there's no point in standing around here."

"Daddy! You said we could go and look at the fishes!" The little girl, who had been standing shyly in the background, spoke up.

"Ava, come and say hello to Nikki," said Cleo

"Hello, Ava." Nikki smiled at her.

Ava twirled around. She had her dark hair tied in two bunches tied with pink ribbons. She had the same beautiful dark brown eyes as her mother and wore a cute pink dress with black tights and bright pink wellington boots, even though there wasn't a puddle in sight. "Hello, Nikki, I'm nearly five. My favourite colour is pink," Ava announced, then pointed to the little boy who was fast asleep in the pushchair. "This is my brother Riley; he's nearly two."

"Ava, let's take Nikki back home for a slice of the cake you helped me to bake this morning, we can go and look at the fish afterwards. Is that OK?" asked Cleo.

Ava took hold of Nikki's hand. "Follow me," she said, making everyone laugh.

They walked up a short path which led to a small, gated estate containing four large, modern houses and a bungalow all built from red brick. Mike tapped a code into a pad built into the wall and the door opened for them. Next to that were the larger double gates to allow cars to enter and exit. Just inside the gate was a small rustic cottage.

"We use this cottage for visiting family and friends," said Cleo.

Ava ran ahead. "We live at number three," she called out.

"What a wonderful safe environment for the children," said Nikki.

Cleo nodded. "We love it here."

"Paul lives in the first house," said Mike, pointing across as they walked. Paul's brother Tom lives at number two, then their parents Richard and Janet live at number four. Their older sister Ruth stays there when she's home on leave. She's a medical doctor working with the charity Medicin San Frontieres. The bungalow is a contingency plan just in case Richard and Janet want to downsize in the future."

Nikki nodded as Mike spoke, looking furtively at Paul's house as they walked past hoping that she wouldn't meet him again today.

They walked around to the back of the house where they entered a door leading to a good-sized boot room with plenty of space for shoes and coats. Another door opened out into an enormous open-plan kitchen, dining, living space. There were shiny white tiles on the floor. In the middle of the large white fitted kitchen was an island. Nikki had always hankered after a kitchen with an island. There were two blue sofas at the far end with an enormous television built into the wall. A long pine dining table filled the rest of the space. This beautiful home wouldn't have been out of place in a glossy home magazine. Nikki smiled at a wall covered with paper where there were splotched handprints and pictures drawn with crayons. There were so many toys around too. It was a lovely family home. She admired the photographic artwork on the walls. There were white sandy beaches looking out to the clear blue ocean. Other photos showed cities lit up at night.

"I love these!" she said. "This whole place is wonderful!" She had worked in some very grand houses, but the design and layout of this house beat them all hands down.

"Cleo is a much in demand interior designer," said Mike proudly while putting Riley who had just woken up into his highchair. The little boy rubbed his eyes and looked suspiciously at Nikki. She waved at him, and he gave a sweet smile which melted her heart. Ava had dashed over to the other side of the room and was already lost in a world of her own playing with her toys.

Cleo laughed. "I've tried to take as long as I could for maternity leave, but I'm starting to get some tentative enquiries. I've been working with Mike and Paul to help to design some areas of the Folly."

"It's certainly unique. I really admire Paul's vision." Nikki furrowed her brow. "Do you think we've lost the contract to work here now? I've got eight guys ready to travel down tomorrow so I'll need to let them know," she asked fiddling with her ponytail again while looking anxiously across at Mike and Cleo.

"I honestly doubt it," Mike replied. "Let me go and speak to him." He kissed Cleo and left the same way they had all come in.

Cleo made Riley and Ava a sandwich and a glass of milk, with a pot of tea and slices of cake for herself and Nikki.

"Come and sit down." She smiled. "I'm sure everything will turn out alright." They sat on comfortable padded high stools at the breakfast bar.

"Is this whole project a family concern? It's quite unusual to find a whole extended family living so close together." Nikki took a bite of the sponge cake. "Wow, this cake is amazing."

"I made it with Mummy." Ava beamed.

"It really is a family business." Cleo said as she poured out the tea. "Paul and Mike are cousins and set up a property development firm as soon as they left university. At the time Paul was a wannabe writer, but Mike loved getting his hands dirty knocking down walls and turning some grotty old places into lovely homes. Fast forward fifteen years and with the money to back it up, Paul wanted to fulfil his dream of creating a place like this. Once they had developed the conference centre, they had the time, space and money to develop the folly."

"I love it. It's going to look wonderful once it's all finished." Nikki sighed. She really hoped that Mike would come back with good news for her, she really wanted to work on this project.

Cleo nodded in agreement. "It's so different and quirky, I'm sure it will attract a lot of interest from artists and writers alike. Paul's younger brother, Tom, is a lawyer and manages all the contracts and legal stuff associated with the business."

"I guess it's easy to forget everything that goes on in the background."

"Absolutely! Richard and Janet, Paul's parents have backgrounds in health, safety, and HR so they will be running that side of things here. They're wonderful people. When Mike and his sister Paris were children their parents were killed in a car crash. Richard and Janet took them in to grow up with their cousins, they're all incredibly close."

"They sound lovely." Nikki's family was not close at all.

"Oh, they are. I'm sure you'll meet them in the next day or so," Cleo replied.

"Is there a significant other in Paul's life?" Nikki flushed and regretted asking the question.

Cleo smiled. "There was. He was with Valentina for three years. She was incredibly high maintenance and insisted on expensive holidays, clothes, and cars. We could all see that she was a gold digger, but Paul was completely taken in by her beauty and she knew all the right things to say to make him feel special."

"Oh dear, so what happened, then?" asked Nikki.

"Paul found out that she had been involved with someone else for most of the time they had been together, and he sent her packing." Cleo shook her head, remembering how devastated Paul had been when he discovered the truth. "She broke his heart, and he hasn't seen or heard from her since, as far as I'm aware. Paul has avoided any relationships ever since."

"I don't blame him." She hated to hear of anybody being taken advantage of. Something inside her felt pleased to hear that he was single although she still felt very angry with his pretence.

"So how about you?" Cleo asked. "Are you single?"

Nikki nodded. "I've been divorced for just over two years. My best friend is Amanda. Her family moved in next to ours when I was five and we've been friends ever since. Her brother Harry is two years older than us and was always part of my life growing up. Harry and I both went to the same university, and while we there, our friendship grew into something more romantic. When he graduated, Harry got a job close to the university as I had a couple more years to go. Once I graduated we got married."

"So, what went wrong?"

"Well, after a couple of years we decided to start a family. Nothing happened and the doctor conducted tests and he couldn't find anything wrong with either of us. After that I became a bit of an ovulation monster. Normal lovemaking turned into a schedule with windows of opportunity. In the end we were having constant arguments and eventually we decided that our marriage had run its course," Nikki replied. It had been emotionally draining towards the end of her marriage and she had steered clear of developing new relationships since.

"I'm sorry. I guess you lost a husband and a friend."

Nikki shook her head. "Not altogether. Although I haven't seen Harry since the divorce, we parted as friends. Once the decision to separate had been made, the friction disappeared at once."

"You're luckier than most I would say," replied Cleo just as Ava came running over.

"Mummy, when can we go and see the fishes?" she asked jiggling about impatiently.

"Daddy has just popped over to see Uncle Paul. As soon as he gets back we'll go out," replied Cleo.

Paul's cage had indeed been rattled. As soon as Nikki had mentioned the disappointing plotline he realised that something had gone seriously wrong.

He picked up his mobile phone which he'd left on the hall table and saw that there were numerous missed calls and messages from his agent Anna Moore. He called her straight away. Anna answered at once.

"Oh, Paul, there's been a dreadful mistake. Your first draft was sent out to the printers and the digital stores in error. I'm so sorry. We've started the recall process. The book is no longer available for download and the bookstores have been told not to sell the copies they've received."

Paul had a unique way of writing; he would create the bones of the story as the first draft which he would then send to Anna so that she could organise the artwork for the cover.

He would then weave in new characters to create the story twists he had become famous for.

"Yeah, I found out from one of my readers just now that something wasn't right." Paul doodled on one of the many notebooks he kept around the house just in case any ideas for new stories sprang to mind.

"Again, I'm so sorry. On a positive note, we think that we've got in quickly with damage limitation and we're preparing a press release to explain the error and of course offering the exchange once we get the correct copies printed. I hope this won't affect our working relationship going forward," her voice faded out and Paul could tell that Anna was trying not to cry.

His foul mood drifted away. He had worked with Anna for over ten years. She was efficient and most importantly she understood the way he liked to work.

"Anna, of course we'll continue to work together!" he replied, and he could feel her anxiety dissipating down the phone. "You sound like you're on top of things. I'll put out a statement on my social media too. No publicity is bad publicity."

"Thank you so much, and I'm very sorry," said Anna gratefully.

"Stop apologising. How long until the new print run can be carried out?"

"The printers are going to prioritise it and the first run should take place this afternoon. Stock levels should be back up to normal by the beginning of next week." Anna was back into business mode.

"You never know, the copies that are out there now might become collector's items in the future," joked Paul.

"I don't think you're wrong there."

The doorbell rang. OK, Anna. I've got to go now, someone's at the door. Bye for now." Paul walked up to the front door as he finished his call with Anna; he could see that it was Mike standing there. "Bye, Paul, thank you for being so understanding."

Paul opened the door. "Hi, Mike, everything OK?" He sounded a lot more like his normal self without any sign of his earlier mood. "Are you OK now? You seemed to be having a major hissy fit earlier and I have Nikki at our house worrying if she's lost the contract we'd given her," Mike said.

Paul felt rotten then. Nikki had been so enthusiastic about the Folly and had proclaimed herself to be one of his biggest fans. Stupidly he had allowed her to go on thinking that he was Mike, interested to hear somebody else's opinion of the project without fear of offending Paul Archer. It had all been sheer vanity and he knew he was wrong to have done that.

"Sorry, mate, I'll come back to your house now and explain." He stepped out of the door to join Mike outside.

31

"And apologise. I can't believe you pretended to be me. What were you trying to achieve by doing that?"

Paul shrugged had looked down at the floor. "I wanted an unblinkered opinion of the folly I suppose. Stupid really."

Mike raised his eyebrows. "Did you pretend to be me when you met Darren the plumber or Anton the builder's foreman?"

They both burst out laughing at that question. "I guess I just saw a pretty girl standing in front of me who thought I was you and thought I would run with it," said Paul as they reached Mike and Cleo's house.

Paul cringed when he saw Nikki visibly shrink as they entered the kitchen. He was sorry to have upset her.

"Uncle Paul!" shouted Ava, who came running over and he picked her up and swung her round making her giggle with delight. He put her down again and she ran straight back over to her toys.

He turned to speak to Nikki, who was watching him warily. "Hi, Nikki. Look, I'm so sorry I was rude earlier. When you pointed out the plot weakness in my latest book I realised straight away that something had gone wrong. Turns out that my publishing company sent a first draft out instead of the right one. It's all getting sorted out now," Paul said. "And I'm really sorry I lied about who I was, it was childish and stupid."

Nikki smiled and her whole face lit up. She wasn't wearing any makeup she didn't need to. Nikki really was an attractive woman.

"Thank goodness!" she exclaimed. "I didn't like to think that you'd got lazy with your writing. I can't wait to read the real thing."

"I promise you'll get the very first copy, with a dedication to you from the author." He grinned back at her. "And of course, you haven't lost the contract."

Nikki sighed with relief. "Thank you, I was so worried about letting the other guys down, and my dad of course."

"So, is your team going to be staying in the contractors' accommodation at the other side of their car park?" asked Cleo as she loaded the plates and cups into the dishwasher.

Paul and Mike had rented some large static caravans for all their contractors when they had bought Burbridge Hall. It had made sense to make life easier for everybody as it was quite a way out from the nearest town. They had decided to keep them for the new set of contractors working on Archer's Folly.

Nikki nodded. "Yes, that will save us a lot of commuting time." She sat back down on her stool.

"Are you the only female?" Cleo asked, tapping her fingers on her chin thoughtfully.

"Well, normally there are three of us, but Wendy has just had a baby and Lou isn't very well at the moment," Nikki replied.

Cleo turned to Mike and Paul. "I think Nikki should stay at the gate cottage. It will be a lot nicer for her there and I'm sure the guys won't want their boss staying with them," she said.

Mike hugged his wife. "That's a great idea," he said and turned to Nikki. "Would that be OK with you?"

Nikki didn't take too long to think about it. She got on well with the guys on her team and they always treated her with the greatest of respect, but she knew that they would be more relaxed if she stayed at the cottage. "That would be fantastic, thank you so much," she replied with a smile.

Nikki was looking forward to the next few months working at Archer's Folly and she hoped she would get the chance to get to know Paul a bit better.

CHAPTER THREE

It was another beautiful morning when Nikki drove through the double gates in her post box red Mini and parked up in front of the tiny cottage. The van she had driven yesterday was going to be used by Matt her trusted second in command to drop off all the equipment and materials.

Feeling a little like she was on holiday Nikki turned the key in the front door and smiled at the scene in front of her. Everything had been finished to an incredibly high standard. From the rustic light oak flooring to the beautiful stone fireplace with spotlights and a wood-burning stove. There was an attractive overstuffed blue and white fabric sofa with matching armchair and a lovely oak coffee table. Pretty crystal wall lights were set around the room. In the corner, a cream carpeted staircase with white painted bannisters led up to a gorgeous bedroom with double aspect windows providing amazing views of the folly. The space had been fully utilised with some fitted wardrobes. In the bathroom there was a free-standing white, natural stone bath facing the window with a view over the rolling countryside beyond. Fluffy white towels were rolled up in a large wicker basket. Everything was perfect. Back downstairs she went through the door at the back of the sitting room leading to a bespoke fitted kitchen in duck egg blue with white tiles on the floor and walls.

A hat box full of fragrant and colourful roses with sprigs of eucalyptus and rosemary sat on the small white wooden dining table. They looked and smelled amazing. There was a small envelope which she eagerly opened. It was a message from Paul. It simply said. *Fresh Start?*

Nikki sighed and the butterflies in her stomach worked overtime.

She thought about the lovely dimples that appeared on his face when he smiled, and those intensely blue eyes and she felt her heart start to beat just a little faster. But she would have to maintain a professional relationship with him. She put some milk, a bottle of wine and some other bits and pieces into the fridge, then popped the rest of her shopping away in the cupboards.

There was a knock at the front door, and Nikki smiled with pleasure when she saw Cleo, Ava and Riley standing there.

Ava carefully carried a plate covered with silver foil. "We've made you some brownies," she announced proudly as Nikki took them from her.

"Thank you so much, Ava. I'm sure they'll be delicious, especially as you made them," replied Nikki and the little girl beamed. "Cleo, this place is wonderful! Thank you so much for suggesting I could stay here."

Cleo smiled at Nikki's enthusiasm. "It made perfect sense for you to stay here, I'm glad you like the cottage," she replied, holding Riley's hand as he walked into the cottage.

"Hello!" he said with a toothy grin and Nikki's heart melted. He really was a lovely little chap. "Come out to the kitchen, I'll put the kettle on," she said.

"That sounds fab," Cleo replied, then stopped to admire the flowers.

"They're from Paul," Nikki said blushing. "An apology for yesterday."

Cleo smiled knowingly and sniffed the fragrant flowers. "Well, that was nice of him." "Ava, Riley, would you like some juice to go with these lovely brownies?" Nikki asked.

"Um, maybe not the Prosecco." Cleo laughed at the bottle Nikki had taken out of the fridge. Nikki blushed flustered by Cleo's reaction to the flowers. "Oops, silly me," she said and found a couple of plastic beakers in the cupboard for the children to drink out of.

"Mike will be over shortly to talk to you about your team's first day tomorrow. You'll all have to have a health and safety induction in the morning with Richard." Cleo helped Ava to take off the foil covering the brownies.

Nikki had almost forgotten she was there to work for a moment, the cottage was lovely, and Cleo was so welcoming. "Absolutely. The guys should all be here by early afternoon, and I'll be going over to see them then."

Mike knocked on the kitchen door and let himself in. "So, this is where my family are all hiding out." "We made Nikki some brownies," Ava replied with chocolate round her mouth and offering the plate to him.

"Mm, these look delicious." He popped one into his mouth.

"Cleo has just told me about the induction tomorrow morning. Would you like to walk over with me to meet the guys this afternoon?" asked Nikki.

Mike nodded. "Sounds like a plan. We can take them for the tour so that they can see where they'll be working. Now who would like to play on the new swing set I have just been putting up in the garden?"

Ava screamed so loudly Nikki had to rub her ears. "Daddy, let's go now!"

"Now!" Riley copied his sister.

Nikki chuckled. "Have fun guys and I'll see you later, Mike," she said as the family all started to leave through the kitchen door. Cleo hugged her and Nikki knew she had made a real friend. The cottage certainly seemed quiet when they all left.

As planned, Mike called for Nikki just after lunch and they decided to walk as it was such a pleasant day. Mike pointed to a Portakabin close to the castle.

"That's my office for the time being. I like to have a meeting every morning at 8 o'clock with all the lead contractors. This week it will be you, the plumber whose team is working on the castle and the lead fitter for the bathrooms and kitchens in the artisan apartments," he said.

"I'll be there promptly every day," promised Nikki.

It was a beautiful afternoon and very warm for the end of April. Nikki was glad she had put on a pair of light blue cropped trousers and a white sleeveless blouse. Her trademark ponytail kept her neck cool. The white marble of the Folly glistened in the sun as they walked past. It was so serene and restful. As they reached the artisan square, they jumped into a golf buggy and Mike drove up the service road to the contractor's car park. Nikki was relieved to see the van's belonging to her team, and they could hear the laughter as they walked towards the caravans. Nikki knocked on the door of the one making the most noise and Matt answered the door. "Hello, Nikki," he said, and he turned around to speak to the guys inside. "Nikki's here, we need to go outside for a chat."

The guys wandered out nodding at Mike and Nikki.

"Hello, everybody, welcome to Archers Folly. This is Mike Dean who is the project manager here." She looked around to make sure that her whole team was present.

"Hi, all," said Mike. "Please jump into the golf buggies and follow us for the guided tour. Nikki will tell you what needs to be done as we go round."

After a lot of banter between the guys around who would be driving the buggies, they drove in convoy around the Folly, Nikki smiled to herself as she heard her team's reactions. This would undoubtedly be the strangest place any of them had ever worked in. But, once they got down to business and she chose the teams for each area she was proud to see how receptive they were to the work that they would all have to do. They all understood how important the Archer's Folly contract was for Nikki's dad, Chris.

As the tour came to an end, Mike stopped his buggy. He pointed out some storage areas closer to the courtyard and the cottages. "Right, guys, I suggest that you spend the rest of the afternoon transferring all of your equipment over here so that you can hit the ground running after your induction in the morning. You can drive your vans on the service road here."

Nikki spoke up, "Don't forget the induction is at eight thirty tomorrow morning so don't be late for that please." Her team all nodded in agreement.

Mike was impressed with the respect that the guys had for Nikki. Cleo really liked her too and that was good enough for him.

The next morning after a very brief eight o'clock meeting, Nikki headed off towards the artisan square where the site induction was due to take place. Today she was wearing a pair of dark blue dungarees with a pink T-shirt underneath ready to make a start on the cottages. She heard somebody walking to catch her up and looked round. A clean-shaven Paul strode towards her, so she stopped and waited for him. He was even more gorgeous without the beard and crazy hair. "Good morning, Paul, I was hoping to see you. Thank you so much for the beautiful flowers, I love them," she said trying to stop her voice from sounding over-excited.

Paul smiled at her and the dimples in his cheeks appeared. Just the sight of them made her heart pound. The fluttering in her stomach intensified. No man had ever made her feel quite like this before. "So, what happened to all the fuzz?" she asked with a broad grin on her face.

"Well, when my super-fan told me that she didn't recognise me, I knew it was time to smarten up a bit. I can't let the fans down."

Nikki gave him a friendly punch on his arm. "Idiot!"

"You're not the first person to tell me that I'm afraid. Anyway, how would you fancy coming out for dinner with me tonight to celebrate your arrival at Archers Folly and the disappearance of my facial fuzz?"

Nikki looked at Paul's expectant face and his piercing blue eyes, and although she had decided to keep things entirely professional, found herself saying, "I'd love to, what time?"

"I'll pick you up at eight if that's OK with you," he replied.

Nikki nodded. It was more than all right with her. They walked in companionable silence until they reached the square where a man who was undeniably Paul's father was chatting to Matt. He looked very distinguished and had the same dimples in his cheeks as he smiled at her and reached out to shake her hand.

"Hi, Dad, this is Nikki Pembroke, she's in charge of the decorating team. Nikki, this is Richard, my father, who is the health and safety manager of the hotel, conference centre and Archer's Folly."

"Hi, Richard, lovely to meet you," she said glancing around the square and seeing that the whole of her team was now present and ready for the induction.

Paul stepped up onto the base of the fountain. "Good morning, everyone, I'm Paul Archer and welcome to Archer's Folly. I know this all looks a bit surreal, but I wanted to create a place which was different to the normal world. This is going to be somewhere where writers and artists can feel both chilled and inspired. I've often had writer's block and have had to take myself away to give my mind somewhere to relax and I hope this will help others to do the same. I also wanted to create a space for different arts and crafts to flourish hence why we built this square. The units in this here will soon be filled with different craftspeople. We have glass artists, a silver jewellery maker, a floral artist, and a woodcarver signed up already with more to follow. I can't wait until everything is up and running. Anyway, I'll hand over to my father Richard who will take you through your induction. Thank you."

Paul smiled over at Nikki before he left the courtyard, and she felt the butterflies start up all over again. She felt inspired by his short speech, he was so enthusiastic about the Folly.

By lunchtime, Nikki had become totally immersed in painting the exterior of one of the cottages. She was using a pastel green and she loved bringing the cottage to life. She looked over at Derek who had worked for her dad for years painting the opposite cottage in pink.

"Having fun over there?" she called over to him.

Derek nodded. He was the same age as her father and had been a family friend for as long as Nikki could remember. He was a quiet chap, tending to keep himself to himself, but the younger guys respected him and the fatherly advice he would hand out from time to time.

"It's different for sure. Now, Nikki, about your night out with Paul Archer this evening. In the absence of your father, I just want you to take care and don't get yourself hurt. Men like that attract women all the time and rarely settle down. Do you understand what I'm saying?" He frowned at her.

Nikki flushed, at once regretting telling Derek about her dinner date. He was like an uncle to her, so it was sweet the way he cared. The advice came from a good place.

"Don't worry, Derek, I'm not about to marry him." She smiled.

A few hours later and the nerves had really kicked in. She had popped one of the beautifully fragrant bath bombs which had been thoughtfully left in a small basket in the bathroom and had enjoyed a relaxing time in the bath. Nikki had stressed over what to wear. She hadn't brought a huge wardrobe with her as she hadn't expected to be socialising much during her time at the folly, but she wanted to look her best. Derek's words had resonated with her. She was sure Paul had dated many stunning women that she couldn't expect to compete with.

It's just dinner, she reprimanded herself and settled on a blue printed midi dress with white sandals and her trusty white bolero jacket. Nikki let her blonde hair flow loosely over her shoulders, a pleasant change from her uniform ponytail. She never generally used much makeup and just used a flick of mascara and a nude lipstick. Simple silver drop earrings were matched with an engraved silver bangle. She checked her watch; it was time and her heart thudded hard in her chest. This was the first time she had been out with anyone since Harry. A car pulled up outside and there was a knock at the door. Nikki took a deep breath and opened it. Paul, dressed in a blue shirt that matched the colour of his eyes and light grey trousers gave a small bow. "My lady, your chariot awaits!" he announced.

Oh, boy! What a chariot too! Nikki thought as she walked up to the blue Aston Martin.

As Paul drove through the country lanes towards Honesty the conversation flowed easily about the folly. He soon pulled up outside an Italian restaurant called La Casa di Costello and reached behind his seat to pick up his jacket. He walked quickly round to open Nikki's door for her. As she got out she inhaled the citrus musk of his cologne, it smelt divine.

"You look beautiful tonight" Paul murmured against her ear as he took her hand and led her to the door of the restaurant where the owner Giovanni was waiting to greet them.

"Welcome, Signor Archer and your beautiful lady." He smiled and took them to a private table for two at a window which overlooked a beautiful garden festooned with pretty fairy lights.

Nikki felt spoilt for choice when she perused the menu and opted for a simple Caesar salad to start with, and they both decided to have the tuna fillet for their main course. Paul had chosen a bottle of Chablis Grand Cru and Nikki loved the crisp citrus flavour.

"So, Nikki, tell me all about yourself. Have you always worked for your father?" Paul asked.

Nikki shook her head. "I have a degree in fine art and after university I became an art teacher," she replied enjoying the look of surprise on his face.

"Wow! I wasn't expecting you to say that. Now I can see why you were so enthused with everything at the Folly." Paul reminded himself he should never judge a book by its cover.

"Oh definitely, it's going to be a wonderful place for artists and writers alike."

"So, tell me your story. How did you end up working at the folly?"

Nikki took another sip of her wine, collecting herself before telling her story. "I married Harry, one of my childhood friends straight after university. We settled down in Kent, I taught at a local art college, and he worked as a stockbroker in the city." Nikki sighed and looked out of the window as if she was composing herself.

Paul reached across to take her hand.

"You don't have to say any more, I don't want you getting upset," he said reassuringly.

"No, it's fine. Long story short, we tried for a family, it didn't happen, and we decided that we were much better off as friends than a couple. I haven't seen him since the divorce two years ago now."

"I'm sorry," said Paul.

Nikki shrugged. "It just wasn't meant to be I guess."

Paul wasn't sure if she was referring to her marriage or the fact that she hadn't had a baby, a mixture of the two he supposed. He topped up Nikki's wine and gestured to the waiter for a bottle of water, he was driving after all.

Nikki absentmindedly stroked his hand as she continued with her story. "Shortly afterwards I moved back to live with Dad. It was becoming obvious that the arthritis was becoming more and more of a struggle for him, so I took over a lot of the workload, and, well, here we are."

"Here we are indeed."

Nikki decided to lighten the mood. "So, lets raise our glasses to absent beards and scruffy hair."

Paul chuckled as they clinked their glasses. "Tell me more about your art."

Nikki's face lit up as she started to talk about her beloved art. "Well, I sketch in charcoals and paint with oils. Last year I reconnected with Scarlet, a friend from university who now owns an art gallery in Cambridge with her husband. They want me to hold an exhibition of my work there in November."

"That's amazing!" enthused Paul. "You must be really good to warrant your own exhibition. You should paint the folly too and add it to your collection."

Nikki grinned. "That's a great idea! I might just do that."

They waited while the waiter cleared the table and returned with the dessert menu.

"So, this morning you mentioned that you took yourself off-grid when you got writer's block. Where do you normally go?" Nikki was interested to find out how Paul produced his impressive plot lines.

Well, I really struggled with the latest book. Halfway through I literally couldn't work out where it was going so I rented a croft on a small Scottish Island and stayed there for the best part of three months," said Paul. It also wasn't long after he had broken up with Valentina and he had just wanted to get away, killing two birds with one stone. "Maybe that's where all the confusion came from, I had sent the first draft over to Anna but needed to get away to work my magic."

"I'm looking forward to reading it once the correct draft is published."

"Thanks, It took a few weeks of staring out at nothing but waves crashing against the rocks, but I got there in the end."

Nikki didn't want their dinner date to end, she had never connected with anybody like this before, not even Harry she felt ashamed to admit. They had decided against ordering dessert but had ordered some coffee. Finally, Paul had paid the bill, and the drive home seemed to pass too quickly. The car pulled up outside the cottage and once again he dashed round to open the car door for her.

"You, Paul Archer, are the perfect gentleman," Nikki said, kissing him lightly on his cheek.

"Come here." He pulled her closer to him and kissed her until fireworks were exploding in Nikki's heart. Reluctantly he let her go, he had also felt a connection to her. He had dated a lot of women, most a lot more sophisticated than Nikki, but there was just something about this beautiful, unassuming woman that piqued his interest. "But you're quite right, I am a perfect gentleman." He walked Nikki to the front door.

"Thank you for an amazing evening," she whispered to him as he lowered his lips to hers for a final kiss.

"Believe me. The pleasure was all mine." He returned to his car for the short drive up to his house.

"Goodnight, Paul," Nikki said softly to the night air as she closed the door, hoping there would be another date again in the future. She heard the notification of an arriving text on her phone.

It said. *Let me cook for you on Saturday night.*
Can I bring anything?
Just yourself xx

Nikki floated on air as she walked up the stairs. Could this be the start of something special?

CHAPTER FOUR

The rest of the week passed quickly with Nikki just seeing Paul in passing as she continued her work on the cottages. They were looking incredible, the mixed pastel colours really making them stand out. Her team was working to the schedule, and they would be ready to move to the artisan square apartments as soon as the kitchen and bathroom fitters had finished.

Saturday arrived and it was a beautiful sunny day. Nikki's stomach was churning, looking forward to her evening with Paul. She had to calm herself down and the best way she could do that was to draw. Nikki pulled on a pretty, lime green sundress with a denim jacket and a pair of white chunky trainers. She picked up her art bag with her sketchbook and charcoals and decided to go down to the folly to make some sketches in preparation for her painting.

Having picked up a bottle of water and made a quick sandwich to take with her Nikki left the cottage and wandered over to sit on one of the benches at the side of the lake. Soon, she was totally immersed in her drawing. It had been far too long since she had last drawn or painted. Life had been so busy over the last few months. It would be fabulous if she could get the painting of the folly done in time for her exhibition in November.

Deciding to take a quick break for lunch, Nikki thought about Paul's family. Mike, Cleo, and the kids were lovely. Richard had quickly earned the respect of her team during the induction, and she could see that Paul would look very distinguished when he was older. She was yet to meet Paul's brother Tom or his mother Janet but, living at the cottage, she was sure to bump into them eventually. Nikki loved it here, it was such a lovely quiet and calm place to be. Just as she was preparing to continue with her sketching, her phone rang. It was Mike.

"Oh, Nikki, thank goodness. Where are you?" He sounded panicked.

"I'm just down at the folly sketching, what's the matter?" she asked, worried by the desperation in his voice.

"Could you come back up here to the house? Riley's fallen off the swing and we need to take him to the hospital. Would you be able to look after Ava for us? Everyone else has gone out."

Nikki had quickly started to put everything away in her bag while she spoke to Mike, she could hear the stress in his voice. "On my way," she replied.

Nikki dashed up towards the gates. Mike had already driven down from their house and had parked up outside the double gates to wait for her while Cleo tried to console a screaming Riley in the back of the car. Ava was sobbing too.

"Look Ava, Nikki's here. She's going to look after you while we get Riley fixed up again," said Mike as Ava clung to him sobbing. "No, Daddy, I want to go with you and Mummy!" she wailed.

Mike rubbed his forehead with his hand and his eyes were wide open in panic. He really needed to get going to the hospital, this was the first time one of the children had been really hurt.

"Come on, Ava, let's go and draw a get well soon card for Riley and make him some biscuits." Nikki said and Ava stopped howling for a moment as she thought about it.

"OK."

Nikki gave her a big hug while Mike mouthed his thanks over his daughter's head as he got back into the driver's seat. The car sped off and Ava's chin started to wobble again. Nikki held her hand and quickly tapped in the code to allow the door to open. They were indoors in no time and Nikki took Ava straight through to the kitchen.

"Have you had any lunch?"

"No, Riley got hurt just before Mummy was going to make lunch," Ava replied.

"How about a cheese and tomato sandwich?" Nikki asked. "And while I'm making that you can have a think about what you would like to draw for Riley. Use this paper and I will let you use my special pastel colouring pencils."

Ava looked impressed at the posh pencils and hummed to herself as she drew something on the paper. After a few minutes Nikki put a sandwich along with a beaker of milk down on the table. She glanced over at Ava's drawing, then studied it again with even more interest. Ava had drawn a picture of her family, and yet for a four-year-old, the detail was astounding. Most children of that age would draw bodies facing forward with arms sticking out at the sides and basic facial features. Ava had cleverly captured Mike's designer stubble and Cleo's beautiful hair. She had drawn herself and Riley standing in between their parents holding hands. She was clearly going to develop into an exceedingly good artist.

"Ava, this is really, really good," she said, and Ava carefully put the pencil she was using down.

"Will you help me to write get better soon Riley at the top of the picture?" Ava reached out for her sandwich.

"Of course, I can. Riley is going to love this, especially as it was drawn by his clever big sister," replied Nikki as she sat down opposite Ava holding a cup of tea.

A little while later there was a tap on the kitchen door and Nikki's heart thumped when she saw it was Paul. He was wearing a pair of navy tailored shorts with a yellow short-sleeved shirt.

"Hello, lovely ladies."

"Hello, Uncle Paul, Riley's gone to hospital, he hurt his arm."

"I know, darling. I've just spoken to your daddy. The doctors have x-rayed Riley's arm and they're going to put a plaster on it." Paul turned to Nikki. "Mike has suggested that we take Ava to her house just in case they get stuck at the hospital for a while. I know I was going to cook for us tonight but given what's happened, and I hope you don't mind but I thought we could make our own pizza's instead."

"Uncle Paul!" shouted Ava. "I love making pizza. Can we go now, please?"

"Ava, you've just had a late lunch." Nikki laughed.

"But it's so much fun making pizza with Uncle Paul." Ava pouted.

Paul was looking questioningly at Nikki.

"The change of plan is fine," she said firmly. "I'm looking forward to making pizzas, let me bring some pineapple."

Paul grimaced. "Pineapple on pizza? You can't have fruit on a pizza."

Nikki got a tin of pineapple out of the cupboard. "I think you'll find that I can."

Nikki carefully placed Ava's drawing into her bag, and they set off up to Mike and Cleo's house. Paul squeezed her hand as they walked, it all felt so natural.

Paul unlocked the door and Ava dashed in and sat down at her little table. As soon as Nikki gave the picture back to her she fully concentrated on copying the lettering along the top.

"Thank you for not minding about our change of plan," Paul said. looking serious for a moment.

"No problem at all, I just hope Riley's going to be OK."

Paul lowered his voice slightly. "The doctors are going to scan his head to make sure that there's no injury there. That's why they're going to be back a bit later."

"I thought they might do something like that, it's better to be safe than sorry."

"I've finished, Nikki!" Ava ran up to the kitchen, waving the paper in one hand.

"This is brilliant," said Paul, genuinely impressed with Ava's picture.

Ava beamed. "Can we make Riley's biscuits now please?"

An hour later after much laughter and copious amounts of flour and icing finding their way over their clothes and the worktops. the biscuits were ready. Nikki had found some heart-shaped cookie cutters and Ava had covered them with her beloved pink icing. Every now and then when she least expected it, Paul would pull her in for some sneaky kisses and she was convinced that he would be able to hear her heart beating wildly.

They had all mucked in to make pizzas and Nikki was delighted when Ava agreed that pineapple was a delicious topping much to Paul's disgust.

After they had eaten, Ava's eyes had started to look tired.

"How about we get you cleaned up and into your pyjamas and then you can choose a movie to watch?" suggested Paul.

"Frozen!" declared Ava and Nikki could tell by the look on Paul's face that this would not be the first time he had seen that film. She took Ava upstairs to get changed and then, while she was cleaning her teeth, Nikki groaned inwardly as she looked at herself in the mirror. What a state she looked! The windswept hair and flour on her nose were bad enough but her sundress was now covered with splats of pizza sauce and pink icing. Nikki blushed wondering what Paul must have thought of her scruffy appearance.

When Nikki and Ava went back downstairs, Paul had cleaned up, and Cleo's kitchen was sparkling once again. He got the film up on the tv screen. Ava insisted on sitting on Nikki's lap and Paul put his arm around them both. For a moment Nikki imagined what it would be like to sit like this with her own child and quickly told herself off for being so silly. It wasn't too long before Ava fell asleep. Paul stroked Nikki's cheek.

"Are you OK?" he whispered.

Nikki nodded. "It's been fun, Ava's so sweet," she replied. "Despite me ending up looking like a total fright!"

"You look adorable," said Paul with real conviction. "I've met women who wouldn't have entertained the idea of getting good and messy in fun activities."

Nikki pulled a face. "I couldn't live like that. I want to be loved for who I am not how nice my nails or hair extensions look."

Paul stared at her for a moment before smiling. "Nikki, I wouldn't want you any other way."

Just then, Cleo and Mike carrying a sleeping Riley came in through the front door. As soon as they called out a greeting, Ava woke up.

"Mummy! Daddy!" she cried, running over to them both.

Cleo's red-rimmed eyes gave away just how stressful the day had been. Mike looked pale with black circles under his eyes. They both slapped on a greeting smile as Ava dashed towards them.

"Thank you so much for looking after Ava for us, she would have been bored rigid at the hospital. Riley's got a broken arm but fortunately no other injuries," said Cleo.

"It was our pleasure," replied Paul, and Nikki nodded in agreement as she collected her bag ready to leave. Once they were both outside Paul put his arm around Nikki's shoulder. "I have a nice bottle of wine indoors. I think we deserve a drink after our hectic day."

"Sounds good to me," Nikki replied as the butterflies started up again.

Although Paul's house had the same footprint as Mike and Cleo's, it felt different. The large hallway was exceptionally light and bright but with minimal furniture. The kitchen was all chrome with shiny black units and neon blue spotlights. A typical bachelor pad Nikki thought to herself. Paul reached up into one cupboard for the glasses and took the wine out of the fridge. He led Nikki over to a black leather sofa and placed their glasses on the coffee table. She put her art bag on the floor.

"Can I see some of your drawings?" asked Paul, interested to see Nikki's work.

"Sure," replied Nikki. "I was sketching down at the folly this morning before Mike called me." She pulled her sketchbook out of the bag and gave it to Paul, who studied her drawings thoughtfully.

"Nikki, you're exceptionally talented. These sketches are amazing," he said with a smile. "Do you miss teaching?"

Nikki sighed. "I really miss teaching. I used to love seeing the students developing their own styles and interpretations of the subjects."

"Would you be interested in teaching some classes in our art castle? We could fit in around your schedule of course," asked Paul. "You're exactly the sort of person I always imagined working here. Your enthusiasm is infectious, it would be a waste of your talent if you never got the opportunity to teach again."

Nikki's eyes widened. "I would love to teach at the castle! Thank you so much. I'm sure we can work something out around work. Matt always takes the lead when I'm not there." As she spoke a huge smile lit up her face and her eyes glittered.

Paul chuckled at Nikki's excitement. Then he put his arm around her and pulled her towards him and kissed her. At her response, the kiss deepened. She gave an involuntary moan and slid one hand up inside the front of his shirt stroking his chest, feeling his heart beating as fast as her own. Paul groaned and pulled away from Nikki.

"Let's go upstairs," he suggested.

Nikki nodded and allowed him to lead her up the stairs to his bedroom. In her head, fireworks were exploding at what was the start of the most magical night of her life.

CHAPTER FIVE

The next morning when Nikki woke up it took her a moment before she remembered where she was. She felt a bit embarrassed, wondering if Paul would think that she was easy for spending the night with him. Then she thought back on their night of passion. Lovemaking with Harry had never been like that, and for a moment she felt guilty for thinking that way. But it was true. Last night had been incredible. The smell of freshly ground coffee beans floated up from downstairs and Nikki jumped out of bed and walked over to Paul's bathroom where she freshened up. She found a plaid shirt in Paul's wardrobe and put it on before going downstairs.

"Morning, beautiful," greeted Paul, liking Nikki's choice of shirt. He walked around the kitchen island to pull her in for a long kiss. When he released her, he walked over to his huge American fridge freezer. "Eggs benedict?"

"That would be lovely," replied Nikki, pouring herself a mug of coffee and topping up Paul's.

As they enjoyed their breakfast in companionable silence, Nikki, still in her happy fuzzy state imagined this being her life forever. Paul was gorgeous, the house was great but could benefit from some feminine touches and the folly got her creative juices flowing.

"Penny for them?" asked Paul.

"I was just thinking happy thoughts."

"Let's have a day out!" Paul suggested. "There's a lovely meandering walk along the stream on the other side of the folly. We'll take a picnic."

Nikki returned to her cottage and had a quick shower. She sprayed herself with her favourite floral perfume and slipped on a floaty pink maxi dress and sandals. She was glad she had brought some more clothes from home when she had visited her father midweek. Having made some sandwiches, taken some grapes and strawberries out of the fridge and added a bottle of wine into a cooler Nikki was ready to go. A short while later Paul pulled up outside the cottage, this time in a silver Range Rover. He hopped out to put Nikki's bag in the boot. He was wearing a pair of cream cargo shorts and a midnight blue polo shirt. She sniffed, enjoying his musky fragrance.

"Mm, you smell gorgeous," she told an amused Paul.

"Right back at you! You look beautiful."

It was just a five-minute drive up to a public car park along the road from the folly. Paul took Nikki's hand and they walked along a shingle path that ran along the side of the stream surrounded by fragrant lilacs, lupins, and clematis. They ambled along enjoying the glorious weather and Nikki felt calmer and happier than she had for a long, long time. There had been her multiple attempts to get pregnant, the inevitable divorce from Harry and then her father's declining health to worry about. Today there was a new clarity to her life. She was suddenly aware that Paul was speaking to her.

"Hello, earth to Nikki."

"Sorry, I was miles away just then," Nikki replied.

"What was you thinking about?"

"Oh, just happy that most of my problems are behind me now."

Paul squeezed her hand. "I'm glad."

Nikki decided to change the subject. "So, do you have any further plans for the folly or are you going to wait and see how it all pans out?"

"No, I think it will continually evolve," Paul replied. "We still have hundreds of acres of land to use. In fact, you gave me something to consider the first day we met when you said that it would be nice for people like your dad who perhaps can't get out so much to enjoy the folly too. We're going to look at the feasibility of building somewhere for respite care, maybe tie up with a charity for some input."

Nikki turned to look up at Paul's face her eyes shining with happy tears. "That would be brilliant! The folly is such a calm and peaceful place, it would be a perfect environment to build something like that."

Paul nodded. "Originally I was thinking of the Folly just being an artistic and creative retreat. But why not extend it to help others?"

As they continued along the path the only sounds they could hear were the bees moving between the beautiful flowers and the sound of the stream bubbling along beside them. They reached a small stone bridge that flanked the stream at a spot where it had become wider. Halfway across Paul stopped and pointed. "Look, you can see the folly through the trees there."

Sure enough, Nikki could see the sunlight shimmering on the beautiful lake and bouncing off the white marble building.

"I'll be honest," said Paul. "I've been lucky enough to travel all around the world, but I am yet to find somewhere as beautiful as this." His phone beeped and he laughed as he read the message. "My mother has invited us both to a family dinner on Wednesday evening. My brother Tom has just returned from spending some time in Australia. One of his friends moved out there a few years ago and has just got married. Anyway, someone, I'm guessing Cleo has mentioned you, hence the invitation. Would you like to come?"

Nikki blushed. "I would love to join you all, thank you."

Paul quickly typed a response and then they took a slow walk back to the car before retrieving their picnic and settling on a nearby grassy bank overlooking the stream and the luscious green fields beyond.

On Tuesday evening an anxious Nikki phoned Cleo. "I don't know what to wear tomorrow night," she said. She hadn't slept well the night before. Her relationship with Paul was very new. There was still so much to discover about each other. Was it too soon to be introduced to his family as a potential partner?

Cleo laughed. "You're totally overthinking it. They're not landed gentry; they would love you even if you turned up in your pyjamas!"

Nikki exhaled. "I just don't want to let Paul down. You said his previous girlfriend was very glamourous and I'm not like that at all. I want to make a good impression."

"Hey, stop thinking like that," Cleo replied. "Valentina isn't around anymore, and Paul is obviously smitten by you. Stop worrying!"

Nikki was in a world of her own the next day and wasn't her usual chatty self. They had now finished the exteriors of the cottages and had started work on the interiors. The walls inside each cottage were to be painted a light grey and then all the doors, bannisters and skirting boards were going to be painted in the same pastel colour as the exterior. They were going to look fabulous by the time they had finished. Derek was worried about Nikki, hoping that things were still going well in her new relationship with Paul.

"What's the matter with you today Nikki?" It was unlike her not to chat away.

"I've been invited to dinner at Paul's parents' house tonight and I'm worried they won't like me."

"Why wouldn't they like you?" Derek asked.

"Well, I haven't known Paul for long, and I'm just one of the contractors at the folly. I'm aware that they thought his last girlfriend was a gold digger, I just hope they don't think the same about me," Nikki replied.

"Nikki Pembroke, you haven't got a nasty bone in your body!" said Derek. "Don't you dare start thinking like that. Paul likes you and that's all that should matter." Derek put his paintbrush down and walked over to Nikki putting his arm round her shoulders. "You're a lovely person. Just go along and be yourself. It will all be fine, I promise," he said.

"Thanks, Derek." She hugged him back.

Later that day, Nikki returned to her cottage and took a long, relaxing bath. She had decided to wear a yellow polka dot belted dress. It was one of her favourite's and had always drawn lovely compliments when she had worn it in the past. She had just slipped on her sandals when Paul knocked on the door.

"Nikki, you look amazing!" He pulled her towards him for a kiss.

She smiled at him and all her worries drifted away.

They walked up to Richard and Janet's house and the front door opened before they had a chance to knock.

"Hi, Mum," said Paul.

Janet smiled. "And this must be Nikki. I've heard everything about you from Ava!"

"Hello, Janet, thank you so much for inviting me this evening," replied Nikki, handing over a gift bag holding a bottle of wine and some chocolates.

Janet was shorter than Nikki with curly blonde hair and the same intense blue eyes as her son. She had a beautiful, welcoming smile.

The house was decorated in a more traditional fashion and the kitchen had pine cabinets with pots and pans hanging from hooks above the range cooker. It was lovely and homely.

Another man stood up. He was unmistakably Paul's brother Tom. They looked so alike.

"G'day!" he greeted them with a fake Australian twang.

"You've put on a bit of weight overseas, bro." Paul laughed

"And you're starting to go grey," retorted Tom.

Nikki chuckled. She loved the banter. Her sister Jessica was incredibly materialistic and obsessed with her looks, while her brother Stuart was a quiet studious person. There had never been banter amongst the three of them and as they had got older their lives had just gone off in their own direction. She felt some sadness about that.

Cleo and Mike arrived shortly afterwards. Lorna, the daughter of one of Janet's very good friends was babysitting Ava and Riley who had been to tea with Janet and Richard earlier on so they wouldn't feel left out. They loved it when Lorna looked after them, she told them funny stories and they barely noticed when their parents left the house.

The evening was an enormous success. There was much mirth and laughter, and Nikki was made to feel like part of the family. She had never been happier.

"I had a fantastic time," she enthused later when Paul walked her back to the cottage.

"Everyone liked you," said Paul. "It's been a while since they approved of a girlfriend."

Nikki had heard about Valentina from Cleo but had never mentioned her to Paul. "Oh, why?" she asked.

"I was with someone for three years. She was unfaithful and more than happy to spend my money. The only people who could see what was happening was my family and in fairness to them they were always civil to her."

Paul kissed Nikki. "But tonight, was the first time that my mum had ever pulled me into the kitchen to tell me how much she liked someone. You were a big hit all round."

Nikki put her key into the lock. "I'm glad they liked me; they're all really lovely people." She turned to look at Paul. "Sleepover?"

Paul pushed her through the door then gave her a deep kiss that set her whole-body tingling. "I think so," he replied.

They both got up early so that Nikki would be on time for her morning meeting with Mike. Paul read his emails while Nikki prepared some bacon and scrambled eggs for their breakfast.

"Oh, wow!"

"What's up?" Nikki stirred the eggs to stop them sticking to the bottom of the pan.

"The film studio wants to make The Royal Spy into a movie. They want me to go to L.A. to work with the scriptwriters."

Nikki beamed. "Congratulations! That's fantastic news! When will you be going over?" she asked as she plated up their breakfast.

"A few weeks yet I would think. It'll take a while for the contracts and financial side of things to be sorted out. I'll be working with the same scriptwriters as before and I want to make sure that they don't adapt my story so that it's unrecognisable."

"Could that really happen?"

"Absolutely. The film that's currently gracing cinema screens was going to be changed significantly. I really kicked back on that one. It's earned them millions of dollars, so they know better now. Anyway, how would you fancy a nice weekend up in London to celebrate my good news? I'd love to take you to my favourite restaurant."

"I'd love to," said Nikki mentally going through the clothes she had brought with her and thinking that she would have to go back to her dad's house. When she had been married to Harry, they had been to many black-tie events and she had several dresses that would be perfect for the coming weekend. Once Paul had left, she phoned Matt to say that she wouldn't be working today, and she drove over to her dad's house with plans to rummage through her wardrobe.

"Hello, Nik," said Chris, surprised to see his daughter. "Is everything OK over at the folly?" He stood up from his armchair where he had been tackling the crossword in the newspaper.

"Yes, all good," replied Nikki, hugging him. "Paul is taking me for a weekend up in London and I wanted to pick some clothes to take with me."

"Very nice," said Chris as he flicked the switch on the kettle.

"We're celebrating because Hollywood wants to adapt another one of his books into a movie."

"That's great news," replied Chris pleased to see Nikki so animated. He'd been very concerned when she had withdrawn from the world and rarely socialised following her divorce. They sat and enjoyed a cup of tea while Nikki updated him about the work at the folly.

"I'll have to come over and take a look soon," he said.

Nikki nodded. "You really should, you won't believe your eyes when you get there."

She went upstairs to the wardrobe where she kept her evening dresses. There was a beautiful fitted black crepe and lace dress that had cost more than a thousand pounds, it was for a dinner to celebrate Harry being made a director at his firm. Nikki had only ever worn it the once and thought that it would be perfect for this coming weekend. She then pulled out a light blue matte satin off the shoulder cocktail party dress which she had bought around the time that her marriage was falling apart. It had never been worn so Nikki decided that it would the perfect choice to pack too. She selected some of her Agent Provocateur underwear and a pair of Louboutin shoes feeling better prepared now for the weekend ahead.

The following afternoon Paul pulled up outside the cottage in his Range Rover. Nikki dressed in a long shirt and jeans was relieved to see that he was as casually dressed as her for the drive up to the hotel.

"Hello, beautiful," he said before he pulled her close for a lingering kiss. He pretended to struggle with the weight of her suitcase which made Nikki wonder if she had packed too much but as he opened the boot of the car she could see two suit bags and a suitcase. On the drive up to London they talked about the countries they had visited and discovered that they had a shared love for Venice and Florence.

"But Valentina only wanted to shop and go to the finest restaurants, she had no interest in the art and culture whatsoever," he said.

"There's so much to see," replied Nikki. "You've missed out on so much!"

"We should go," replied Paul. "Soon."

Nikki felt like she was in a new and shiny bubble of happiness. Paul was gorgeous, kind and funny. They were discovering that they had so much in common. She was really looking forward to this weekend.

They arrived at the hotel in Mayfair and Paul drove the car down into the underground car park. As they emerged from the elevator a porter immediately rushed over to take their luggage up to the suite that Paul had booked for them. Nikki had never stayed anywhere quite as wonderful as this. The suite was huge and as they walked through the door her feet sank into the most luxurious cream carpet. There were light green, overstuffed chairs and sofas with a dark oak writing table and bureau. An ice bucket containing a bottle of champagne with two beautiful champagne flutes sat on the glass coffee table. Nikki walked through a door into the bedroom which had an emperor sized bed, she sat on the edge of it and looked up at Paul who was enjoying seeing her reaction to everything.

"We'll never find each other in here!" She laid down.

"I think we will," he replied before laying down and kissing Nikki on the neck which made her quiver.

Later, after they had showered together Paul went to sit in the lounge area to give Nikki some time to dress for dinner. He opened the champagne and poured it into the two flutes. As she joined him his mouth dropped open, she looked so beautiful. The black dress clung to her slim body and the black Louboutin patent leather shoes with satin bows screamed class. Nikki had wound her blonde hair up into a bun showing off her diamond-studded earrings and matching choker. In a departure from her usual minimal look, Nikki had created smoky eye makeup with red lipstick.

Paul passed a champagne flute to her. "You look amazing," he said, kissing her.

She smiled, despite spending most of her time dressed in dungarees and overalls, she knew that she scrubbed up well and she enjoyed seeing the effect she was having on Paul.

They went to a nearby French brasserie which had been awarded two Michelin stars where the intimate dining room was lit up only by wall lights and the flickering candles on the tables. The waiter brought their langoustine and caviar starter's to the table.

"Paul, you've achieved so much already in your life, your books are a success, you can afford to stay at wonderful hotels and eat at restaurants like this one. What other ambitions do you have?" asked Nikki as she tried caviar for the first time ever.

Paul took a drink of his wine and looked across at her. "I used to think that I wanted to buy my own yacht and houses all over the world, but the folly idea had been growing for ages and I gradually realised that my priorities lay there. I think the materialistic stuff was more to do with my relationship with Valentina. I'm ashamed to say that I allowed her to drive our lifestyle. At the time it was decadent and fun but after we broke up I found that I didn't really miss it that much at all."

"Sometimes, the simplest things in life are the nicest." Nikki put her fork down. She hadn't really enjoyed the taste of caviar. Paul, on the other hand had eaten his with gusto.

"I have to say, I agree with you now," he replied. "I can't wait for the folly to open, we're just months away from that now, and I'm constantly thinking of new ideas for its expansion going forward."

Nikki waited as the waiter took their plates away. "What sort of ideas have you been coming up with?"

Paul topped up their wine glasses. "My sister Ruth thinks it would be good to set up a rehabilitation centre for injured service men and women. She said that the peace and quiet would be perfect for something like that. My mum thinks that we could build a high-end wedding venue. Honestly with the acreage that we have, the world is quite literally our oyster."

Nikki's eyes sparkled as he spoke, she was looking forward to teaching at the art castle and all these new ideas sounded so exciting.

"So, how about you? What would you like to achieve?" Paul took her hand and rubbed his thumb gently across it.

"I'm excited about my exhibition at the end of the year, not every artist gets that opportunity. Your offer for me to teach at the folly is huge and life-changing for me. Although I'm more than happy to help dad out with the decorating, I know I couldn't carry on with that forever."

The waiter returned with their main courses, a steak in a bearnaise sauce for Paul and a fish stew for Nikki.

"This is my favourite restaurant," said Paul, closing his eyes with ecstasy as the exquisite flavours exploded inside his mouth.

As Nikki ate her bouillabaisse she felt inclined to agree with him.

The rest of the weekend passed like a wonderful dream for Nikki. They wandered round the Tate Modern art gallery and drank cocktails at a rooftop bar which provided views of St Pauls cathedral. Paul had got them the best seats in the house to see Hamilton and afterwards they had eaten at a fabulous Thai restaurant. She would never forget it she had learned so much about Paul and he was genuinely interested in her hopes and dreams too. Nikki was falling hard for Paul Archer.

CHAPTER SIX

The following three weeks passed by with Nikki working on the folly by day and spending her time off with Paul. They went to Hampton Court Palace, Nikki loved it there and Paul had never been, he raved about it all the way home. It had given him inspiration for future builds at the folly. Paul, it turned out was also an amazing cook and she spent many evenings at his house enjoying the lovely food that he created.

Soon it was time for Paul to travel to Los Angeles. "Will you miss me?" He hugged Nikki while they waited for the taxi that was to take him to the airport.

"I really will. But I'm going to use the time to try and finish my sketches of the folly."

On Saturday morning she returned to her favourite bench by the lake to continue her sketching. The artwork was coming along nicely, and she would soon be able to start converting her sketches into the painting she was hoping to be able to include in her exhibition. Nikki also planned to use this area

77

for one of the art courses she was going to run. Her phone rang and she was thrilled to see that it was her best friend Amanda calling.

"Hi, Amanda, how are you?" she asked. "How are Simon and Phoebe?"

Nikki had never really understood how Amanda who was an outgoing, fun-loving person had ended up being married to Simon who was always so quiet and serious. But they were clearly very much in love and Amanda had given birth to their daughter Phoebe just a few weeks before Nikki had left to work at the Folly.

"Hi, Nikkers!" Amanda laughed, using her favourite childhood name for her friend.

"Baby and husband all doing well, thankfully. We don't get a lot of sleep nowadays, but Phoebe is such a good baby most of the time. It's hard to remember life without her now. Anyway, how are you getting on?"

"Oh, I'm having the best time. This is the most unusual place. Paul has designed a whimsical retreat with crooked cottages, a castle, a lake, and an artisan courtyard. I can't wait for it to open up!"

"Paul?" asked Amanda suspiciously. "Are you on first name terms with your favourite author now? I thought he was your boss?"

Nikki blushed, glad that Amanda couldn't see her face. Almost at once this changed.

"I want to see you, put your camera on," she ordered.

Nikki sighed; Amanda knew her so well there would be no hiding place when she spoke about Paul. "Well. We might be in the initial stages of a relationship."

Amanda gave a big beaming smile. "It's about time you started to put yourself out there again. You haven't even been out on a date since Harry have you?"

"No." Nikki sighed. "This is the first guy since Harry." She was so glad that she hadn't lost her close friendship with Amanda after the divorce.

"Are you happy?" asked Amanda.

"Ecstatically. Paul's in America now for talks about another one of his books being turned into a film. He's only been gone two days and I'm really missing him already."

"Aw, sweet. Anyway, about Harry—"

"Is he OK?" Nikki butted in. She would never want any harm to come to him.

"He's fine honestly," said Amanda. "The thing is he's met someone. Melissa. They've just got engaged. He's got it into his head that he wants you to meet her, just to stop any awkwardness at any future gatherings. How would you feel about that?" Amanda looked at her friend, unsure of what the reaction would be, it was a big ask.

Nikki realised that she felt nothing at receiving this news from her friend. Just a calmness. Whether it was something to do with her burgeoning romance with Paul, she didn't know. But yes, she would feel comfortable meeting Harry and his new fiancé now.

"I would be happy to meet up with them both. I'd prefer it if you came along too, just for moral support," Nikki replied, knowing that she couldn't do this on her own.

"Absolutely," agreed Amanda who wanted to support both her best friend and her brother. "Would next Friday evening work for you? Simon is more than able to look after Phoebe for a few hours."

"That would be fine. There's a pub in Honesty called The King's Rest. I'll book a table for seven thirty, would that be OK?" replied Nikki.

"That sounds fab," said Amanda. "But I also want you to visit us to see Phoebe soon. We're looking to have her christened in a couple of months and you are the number one choice for godmother."

"Of course, I'll visit soon, and I would love to be Phoebe's godmother. OK, I'll book the table for Friday. Look forward to seeing you then."

They ended their call and Nikki couldn't help but wonder what Harry's future wife looked like. She would find out next week.

Over the next few days Nikki threw herself into her work. The cottages and the writers building were now complete, and her team was split between the artisan apartments and the art castle. They would be finished in a month, and she felt a lurch in her stomach every time she thought about moving out of the cottage and going back home. She would be teaching at the castle, and it would make sense for her to move closer to the folly, maybe buying a small cottage in Honesty. But then she felt guilty for thinking about moving because she did so much for her dad at home. Paul messaged her several times a day. There was an eight-hour time difference so he did sometimes call her early in the morning which would be late at night for him. Nikki couldn't wait for him to come home again. He'd said that he wasn't sure when, but it wouldn't be too much longer.

Friday arrived and Nikki anxiously thought about the evening ahead. Her stomach had been churning and she had had a headache for most of the day She hadn't seen Harry for two years and hoped she wouldn't feel emotional when she saw him tonight.

Nikki dressed in a pair of skinny jeans and a black and white animal print top. She hadn't heard from Paul that morning, but he had explained the night before that he'd be pretty tied up for the day. Nikki's hands shook as she picked

81

up her car keys from the kitchen table. Her head pounded so she took a couple of painkillers before she left the cottage allowing plenty of time to drive to the pub in Honesty. She was the first one to arrive and was happy to see Mike and Cleo sitting at an outside table.

"Hi, guys," she said. "Date night?"

Cleo nodded. "Yes, Janet and Richard have taken the kids for the night so we're making the most of it. So, tonight's the night that you meet your ex-husband and his new fiancé. How do you feel about it?"

"OK, I think," Nikki replied. "Amanda's coming as well thank goodness. Ah, here they are now." A silver Mondeo pulled into the car park.

"Hope it all goes well," replied Cleo.

Nikki walked down to the car park. Amanda was the first to get out of the car and she threw her arms around Nikki to give her a big hug. "Wow look at you!" exclaimed Nikki. "Nobody would ever guess that you had given birth just three months ago."

Amanda had always been keen on keeping fit and had started to exercise as soon as possible after giving birth to Phoebe. Her blonde hair shone, and she looked happy and contented. Motherhood obviously suited her.

She turned then to face Harry who was waiting anxiously on the other side of the car. He'd really changed since she had last seen him. His ginger hair had always been cut neatly but now it was long and untidy. He wore a loud brightly coloured patterned shirt with distressed jeans and a lime green jacket. He wouldn't have been seen dead wearing clothes like that when they were together.

"Hi, Harry," said Nikki and he relaxed instantly.

"Hello, Nikki," he replied before helping Melissa get out of the car.

As she stood up, Nikki lurched as though she had been shot through the heart. Melissa was heavily pregnant. Her head pounded. *Maybe it was my fault I couldn't get pregnant. The problem really is with me.*

Cleo raised an eyebrow as she watched Harry bring Melissa round to meet Nikki. She had a feeling that her friend would be upset and questioning herself.

Melissa was very tall; her black hair was styled in a pixie cut that showed off her angular features. She wore maternity jeans with a white shirt clinging to her bump. She was quite nervous which was understandable under the circumstances.

"Hi, Melissa." Nikki tried to smile as warmly as possible. Melissa returned an anxious smile. "Let's go inside and find our table." Nikki turned and led the way into the front entrance of the pub.

Once they were settled at their table and drinks had been served Nikki was grateful that Amanda had kept the conversation flowing. She didn't want to appear to be rude, so she spoke up.

"Well, congratulations to you both on your engagement. Have you set the date yet?" She glanced down at Melissa's ring finger and noticed that Harry hadn't presented her with his grandmother's emerald engagement ring that she herself had worn. Instead, she saw a simple solitaire ring although the diamond was huge.

"Thank you," Harry and Melissa replied together. Harry continued to speak, "We're just a few weeks away from when our little boy is born, and we've decided to put the wedding off until next year on his first birthday."

"What a lovely idea," said Amanda with a huge smile. "Phoebe could be your flower girl."

"That would be so sweet," replied Melissa, who had lost her feeling of nerves once she had met Nikki. She hadn't particularly liked Harry's idea about meeting his ex-wife, but she understood his reasoning. Any insecurities she had felt had slipped away once Nikki had spoken about her new relationship with Paul and had felt very comfortable in her presence.

"I'm genuinely very happy for you both," said Nikki and she meant it. She was crying inside for the baby she would never have but good luck to her ex and his new family.

The evening passed pleasantly and as it got dark Amanda decided that they should make a move as they had an hour and a half's drive to get home. Melissa and Amanda said their goodbyes and went to sit in the car.

"Thank you for wishing us well," said Harry. It had been two years since he had seen Nikki and he had been surprised earlier on that evening at the strength of feeling he still had for her. The decision to separate was the right one and he was very happy with Melissa, but he knew that there would always be a special place in his heart for Nikki.

"Harry, we were never meant to be, I see that now. I'm glad that we've remained friends. It would have been horrible to feel uncomfortable at any future family gatherings," Nikki said fervently. She'd been so nervous about seeing him again. The pregnancy had been a terrible shock for her, and she had selfishly felt a deep sadness about it all evening.

"And I'm glad you've met someone, too," said Harry. Nikki nodded. "Thank you. It's still early days but it's really good between us." Harry pulled her closer to him and kissed her lightly on the lips. "I hope everything turns out well for you too. Thank you for meeting us tonight, it meant a lot."

"No problem at all."

Paul hadn't been able to stop thinking about Nikki while he was away and had been able to get through everything

85

necessary to allow him to return home early. He had landed back in the UK wanting to surprise Nikki the next morning. While driving home he had suddenly felt the urge to eat one of the award-winning meat pies that The King's Rest was famous for. He drove into the village and turned into the pub car park just in time to see Nikki kissing another man. He sat there watching as she waved him off and then walked across to her own car. As she opened her driver's door Paul appeared next to her.

"Paul, you're back! What a lovely surprise." She beamed and tried to put her arms around him, then frowned when he pulled back. "What on earth's the matter?" Her heart pounded. Something wasn't right. His face was bright red and contorted in anger.

"You couldn't even wait for me could you?" he hissed.

"What are you talking about?" Nikki frowned. "Of course I've been waiting for you. I've been dying to see you again!"

"I just saw you kissing that guy."

Nikki laughed, which wound him up even further. If that was all that was worrying him she could easily reassure him. "Oh, he was only—"

"I don't care who it was," he butted in not prepared to listen to Nikki's explanation at all. "What is it with the women in my life? Why do I always pick the unfaithful ones?"

Nikki scowled. Why couldn't he just listen to her? It was like he had already made his mind up that she was in the wrong. "Don't be ridiculous, surely you don't mean that? If you could let me explain—" Tears pricked her eyes

"That's what Valentina used to say, "oh Paul, let me explain," Paul replied in a girly sounding voice. He glared at her. He knew what he had seen with and that was Nikki kissing another man. She had been caught out.

Nikki started to cry, with hot tears streaming down her face. This was turning into a nightmare. Paul was totally unprepared to listen to her.

"Oh, that's right, turn on the waterworks. I want nothing to do with you ever again. Just stay away from me until you finish the job then go home and stay home. We're done!" He couldn't believe he had allowed himself to be cheated on again. Paul stormed off, got back into his car, and sped off up the road. Nikki got into her car in a state of shock. She couldn't believe what had just happened. She fumbled in her bag, got her phone out and called Matt, her second in command.

"Hi, Nikki, is everything OK?"

"No, Matt, I need to go home for a while." Her voice wobbling with emotion.

"Is everything OK with Chris?"

"He's fine, it's me. I need to take a time out. We're on schedule at the folly. Can you manage without me for a few days?"

"Of course, we can. Look, is there anything I can do to help you?" Matt had known Nikki for years and was very fond of her. She broke down in tears.

"Please don't say anything to anyone at the folly, just say its family stuff if anybody asks," begged Nikki.

"Consider it done," replied Matt before ending the call.

Nikki sat in her car and sobbed until she had run out of tears. It had all been too much for her. First the shock of Harry and Melissa expecting a child and now the misunderstanding with Paul. She felt so angry with him for not being prepared to listen to her, the explanation would have only taken a couple of minutes and then all would have been well with them. But, he had immediately thought the worst of her and that just made her angry. She started the car and drove the thirty miles home.

It was just after midnight when she put the key in the lock. She crept in quietly not wanting to wake her father up. But there was a light on in the kitchen and when she walked through he was sat at the kitchen table reading a book.

"Hello, love, what's wrong?" he asked when he saw her red and blotchy face.

Nikki sat down at the table with him. She took one look at his worried and concerned face and burst into tears again.

"I've come home, Dad. Paul has just accused me of being unfaithful to him when all he saw was Harry kissing me to say goodbye! He wouldn't even let me explain. I'm so angry with him!"

Chris looked sadly at his daughter as she sobbed. She had been so happy lately and didn't deserve to be feeling like this.

The next day Mike and Cleo were sat outside in the garden with Richard and Janet who had returned Ava and Riley following babysitting duty which had ended with a visit to a nearby petting zoo. It was a gorgeous sunny day again and Mike was preparing to fire up the barbeque. A little while later Paul showed up and they could see straight away that he was in one of his foul moods.

"What's bothering you mate?" asked Mike as Paul plonked himself heavily down into a chair and just sat staring out towards where Ava and Riley were playing.

"Nothing," Paul replied with a scowl. He was still filled with rage at what he had seen the night before. "Jet lag."

Mike and Cleo looked at one another and exchanged knowing glances. They knew that it wasn't jet lag.

"Have you seen Nikki since you got back?"   Cleo asked.

"Nope," replied Paul.

"How was your trip?" asked Janet, feeling quite irritated at her son's juvenile responses.

"Fine, lots of meetings, all good," Paul replied in a voice that made it clear that he didn't want this barrage of questions.

Everyone just left Paul alone after that. When he was in one of his moods there was absolutely no point trying to make any more effort to try and engage him in conversation.

"Anyway, thanks for looking after the kids last night, it was great to go down to the pub for a bite to eat." Cleo loved her children dearly, but it was so nice to get to spend some time alone with Mike.

"No problem," Richard replied. "We love having them over to stay, they're good as gold."

Ava and Riley never played up when they stayed overnight with Richard and Janet who loved having them to stay. They loved to spoil them both when they took them out and about.

"I felt really sorry for Nikki though," Cleo continued. "Her ex-husband Harry had wanted to introduce her to his new fiancé and Nikki booked them all a table at The King's Rest and had asked her best friend Amanda who is also her ex-husband's sister to come along for moral support."

"Isn't that a bit strange for an ex-husband to introduce his new soon-to-be wife?" Janet furrowed her brow.

"Well normally yes," replied Cleo. "But they had all grown up together as family friends and the divorce was civil. There was always a chance that they would run into each other at family parties, weddings, and christenings."

"Makes sense then I suppose," said Janet, unconvinced. She glanced over at Paul who appeared to be taking no notice or interest in what they were saying.

"When his fiancé got out of the car she was heavily pregnant. One of the reasons for Nikki's divorce was because they had tried for quite a long time to have a baby, but it just didn't happen for them, and the stress caused them to split up."

"Oh, the poor girl," said Janet sympathetically. "She must have seen the new partner and thought that it was down to her that she couldn't get pregnant."

"I think that probably was exactly what she must have thought when she saw them last night," said Cleo. Her friend's sad face had haunted her all evening.

Mike chirped up. "Funny looking chap though, he was a real scruff. I honestly would never have put him and Nikki together at all."

Paul groaned and rubbed his face in his hands.

"What's up, Paul?" asked his dad.

"I've been the world's biggest idiot, that's what," he replied in a strangled voice. "I pulled into the car park at the pub last night and I saw Nikki kissing a man who I'm now guessing was her ex-husband. I called her out on it when he drove off and accused her of being unfaithful. Oh, God! I made her cry. What a jerk!"

"You're a complete idiot!" snapped Cleo. "You know Nikki worships the ground you walk on. Why would she two time you just because you were away? She isn't Valentina, she's nothing like her at all. She's a sweet and kind person."

"Why are you cross, Mummy?" asked Ava, who had walked over to investigate the animated conversation.

"I'm not cross, darling, just telling Uncle Paul off for being a silly billy." This made Ava giggle. "Uncle Paul's a silly—" she sang but Janet jumped up. "Come on, Ava, let me push you on the swing," she said firmly.

With a suspicious look at the adults, Ava followed her grandmother to the swing.

Paul stood up looking sheepish. "I've got to put things right," he said before walking away.

He walked straight over to the cottage but there was no sign of Nikki's car. He walked around to the back to look in through the kitchen window but there was no sign of her at all, everything was neat and tidy. He tried to call her several times, but it went straight to voicemail. In the end he gave up, he didn't want to apologise with a message. He would wait until Monday when she was back for work.

Paul couldn't settle down all weekend as the guilt at what he had said to Nikki totally engulfed him. He just laid morosely on the sofa staring at the television without taking any notice of the programmes that were being shown.

On Monday morning Mike turned up at his office ready for the morning meeting to find a dishevelled looking Paul already waiting there. He looked pale with huge black bags under his red-rimmed eyes. He clearly hadn't shaved for several days.

"Have you managed to get hold of Nikki mate?" he asked, feeling concerned for Paul. The last time he had seen him like this was when he had found out about Valentina being unfaithful. This was all self-inflicted though, Paul should have just listened to what Nikki had to say.

Paul shook his head. "Her phone's switched off."

The door opened and he looked up eagerly, but Matt was the only person standing there.

"Hi, guys." He scratched his head. "Um, Nikki has taken some time, she's got family problems at home."

"That's fine, mate," replied Mike. Paul sat at the desk pretending to study some paperwork. "Let her know that if she needs anything she only has to ask."

Matt nodded. "I will, thanks."

After the meeting, Paul jumped up and went through the filing cabinet.

"What are you after?" asked Mike. "Mate, what are you doing?"

Paul was pulling files out and chucking them haphazardly onto the desk. "I need to find Nikki's address; it should be in the paperwork somewhere."

"Just stop!" said Mike. "I have their file here; we were talking about their contract just now at the meeting if you remember."

Paul had not taken any notice at all of what was being said. He took the file from Mike and sat down. He used his phone to take a photo of the address at the top of the headed notepaper and stormed out of the office again without another word.

Mike rolled his eyes as the door slammed shut. When Paul was like this there was nothing he could say or do to calm him down.

Paul walked straight over to his car and typed Nikki's address into his satnav. He drove off tapping his fingers on the steering wheel in irritation as he waited for the gates to slowly open to allow him to drive away.

He needed to make things right with Nikki again. He had been a stupid fool.

CHAPTER SEVEN

Nikki was curled up in the armchair wrapped in her fluffy pink dressing gown. She had hardly slept at all over the weekend and had barely eaten anything which worried Chris a great deal. He walked through with a mug of tea for his daughter.

"Here you go, my love, hot and strong tea with two sugars." He put the mug down on the coffee table and sat on the sofa opposite his daughter.

Nikki gave him a watery smile. "Thanks, Dad," she said in a quiet voice.

"How are you feeling today?" Chris asked.

"Empty," Nikki replied. "I'm so angry with Paul for not believing me. I was starting to fall in love with him, but it would never have worked if he didn't trust me. I wouldn't want to feel like I was walking on eggshells the whole time. His ex-girlfriend has a lot to answer for, but he's going to have to work through some issues before he starts another relationship."

"I'm sorry, love, you've been so happy lately."

"He made me happy, happier than I ever was with Harry."

A pounding came at the front door. They both looked over to the window and saw a silver Range Rover outside.

"It's Paul," said Nikki turning pale and hugging her mug of tea closer to her.

Chris stood up. "You just leave him to me, love."   He walked out into the hall and opened the front door. Paul was standing there with desperation all over his face.

"Mr Pembroke, I'm Paul Archer," he began.

"I know who you are, son, you're the man who has broken my daughter's heart. How dare you accuse her of playing around! Nikki is the most honest woman I know and the kindest. When I lost my wife—" Chris's voice faltered "When I lost my wife, Nikki was my rock, and she's been here for me ever since. Never complaining, giving up her own career to help me. She's been so happy lately; all she could talk about was you. Now she's sitting inside with her heart breaking."

Paul hung his head in shame and when he looked up again there were tears running down his face. "I'm so sorry." He wiped the tears away from his face as he spoke. "I was a total idiot. Please let me speak to Nikki so that I can apologise."

Chris crossed his arms. "Just go, Paul. Leave Nikki alone. My guys can easily manage the rest of the work up at the folly under Matt's leadership. You have some serious trust issues; I'd sort yourself out if I were you."

"Please…" begged Paul as Chris closed the door in his face.

When he walked back into the lounge Nikki was sobbing her heart out.

"Oh Dad, he made me so happy." She threw herself into his arms.

Chris stroked her hair just like he used to when she was a little girl. "I know love, I know," he replied.

Paul got back into his car and buried his face in his hands. He couldn't lose Nikki like this; they were so good together. He was falling in love with her. Just like that he had found the right person for him to share his life with and he had gone and blown it.

Later that day an enormous bouquet of flowers turned up at Chris's house. Nikki couldn't even see her dad's face through the vast array of colourful blooms as he carried it through to her.

"There's an envelope here for you too," said Chris.

Nikki took the flowers and sniffed at the beautiful fragrance. She walked through to the kitchen and placed them in the sink and then opened the back door into the garden. Her mum Stella had spent many, many happy hours creating this beautiful garden bursting with colour throughout the seasons. Nikki walked over to the bench where her mum used to love to sit. "Oh, Mum," she murmured. "I need you so much right now."

Stella had died suddenly when Nikki was fourteen years old. Chris had been devastated by his wife's death and Nikki had ended up playing mum to her sister Jessica and brother Stuart who were ten and twelve at the time.

Nikki opened the envelope recognising Paul's handwriting on the front. She took the letter he had written and started to read.

Darling Nikki,

I can never say sorry enough times to make up for the way I treated you the other evening. I was so wrong to even imagine that you could act the way I accused you of. All my family are furious with me too, I'm an idiot, a stupid bloody idiot!

You are the sweetest, kindest woman I have ever met. We were meant to be together. Archer's Folly would mean nothing to me without you being there. Please give me a second chance to make you happy.

Paul.

"So, what do I do now, Mum?" Nikki sniffed. "Should I give Paul another chance?"

A large, beautiful orange butterfly settled on her knee. After a minute or so it fluttered off again. Nikki smiled as it flew away. "Thanks, Mum, message received."

Paul was back to lying miserably on his sofa when he received a ping on his phone. He glanced at the screen with no intention to responding to anybody when he noticed that Nikki had sent the message. He sat up straight, his hands were shaking as he opened the message.

One more chance! I'll be back tomorrow. N x

"Yes!" He jumped to his feet. For the first time in four days, he realised he hadn't showered, shaved, or even changed his clothes since his return from America. First, he needed to remedy that, then he needed to apologise to his family.

The next day the heavens opened and the windscreen wipers on Nikki's mini were working at full speed to clear the heavy rain obscuring her vision as she drove through the country lanes leading to the folly. As she pulled up in front of the gates she saw Paul standing on the other side holding a large, black umbrella. She drove through, jumped out of the car, and ran to him throwing herself into his arms. He dropped the umbrella and they held each other tightly, oblivious to the rain that was coming down even harder now. The car horn being sounded broke them out of their reunion. Cleo sat in her car grinning.

"Hello, lovebirds. Sorry to interrupt but I need to pick Ava up from preschool. Nikki, could you move your car for me please?" she called through the open window.

Nikki grinned back at her. "Sorry," she called out as she dashed back to her car. She moved out of Cleo's way allowing her friend to drive past. Nikki pulled up in front of the cottage where Paul was waiting. She got out and ran over to open the front door just as a loud clap of thunder rolled around above them. As soon as they were inside they embraced again, and their kisses deepened.

"Let me show you how much I've missed you." Paul pulled her towards the stairs.

A little while later Cleo returned from picking Ava up from her preschool. She had only been attending for a couple of weeks and had already made lots of friends.

"Look, Mummy!" said Ava pointing at Nikki's car. "Nikki's back. Can we visit her?" Cleo smiled to herself. She had a feeling that a visit wouldn't be welcomed right now. "Later, let's get home and out of this rain."

As soon as they got inside the house Cleo put the light on as it was dark outside. There was a very loud clap of thunder which made Ava scream and Riley cry. Suddenly the lights went out, a power cut. A moment later a bright flash of lightning filled the room which made Ava scream again. Then, there was a knock at the door and Richard and Janet walked in totally drenched from their dash across from their house. Cleo felt relieved, hopefully they would be able to help her to distract the children. The large window gave them a view of the folly.

As they looked at the miserable scene outside, Janet gasped. "Oh no, look! The columns of the temple don't look very stable."

With the next gust of wind, the columns swayed before folding in on themselves.

Nikki and Paul appeared from under the duvet when Paul's phone rang.

"They can call back later if it's important," he said, kissing her before she could reply.

Something cracked. Nikki glanced out of the window as the sheet lightning illuminated the outside momentarily making it look as bright as a summer's day. She was shocked by what she saw.

"Oh, my God, Paul something's on fire over past the folly!"

Paul sat up at once just as his phone started to ring again. He answered it holding it under his chin as he pulled on his clothes. It was Mike, but the connection was poor. "Paul...lightning strike... units," was all he could hear Mike saying.

"On my way!" he shouted.

Nikki quickly dressed and grabbed her Hi-Viz jacket and they both dashed downstairs and out of the cottage. Richard and Tom were also making their way towards the gates. They all ran through the heavy rain which soaked them through making their legs feel heavy. The strong gusts of wind whipped against them almost knocking them over. The storm was right above the folly now and forks of lightning split through the low dark heavy clouds as the thunder crashed. As they ran they slipped and skidded on the soggy grass beneath their feet.

High orange flames rose above the artisan square despite the rain. They all stood bent double for a moment trying to catch their breath after the sprint across, tired out from their fight against the elements. All the guys in Nikki's team were looking distressed at what had happened and one or two of them were openly crying. Delegates and staff from the hotel and conference centre had run up to see if they could be of any help and were milling round but Mike walked over and sent them away again. He walked over to Paul and the others.

"Direct hit on one of the larger units, emergency services on their way. Part of the temple on the island has collapsed too," he shouted so that he could be heard above the wind which was gaining strength all the time.

"Is anybody hurt?" asked Paul.

Mike looked down at the ground. "Nikki, I'm sorry but Derek was working in the apartment when it was hit."

"No!" screamed Nikki as she made a move towards the square, but Paul stopped her. "It's too dangerous, we just have to wait now." Her pulled her towards him.

But she wriggled away and ran towards her team. Matt was looking visibly upset and trying to look after the youngest two guys who were still crying with the shock at what had happened. The rest of the team looked dazed and shattered.

"Matt, are you sure Derek was inside?" sobbed Nikki.

He just nodded miserably in response. The sound of sirens could be heard amid the storm and soon the blue lights could be seen as the fire engines, ambulances and police cars drove up towards the folly.

The storm was still strengthening, the wind was so strong it was difficult to stand upright. There was another loud crash, and somebody could be heard faintly shouting above the wind and pointing towards the island. The rest of the temple building collapsed, two of the columns rolling into the lake. Paul's big dream was literally crashing and burning in front of him, he was devastated. Everyone stood silently and watched as the fire fighters started to work at putting the fire out and searching for Derek. It was obvious that nobody could have survived the lightning strike and ensuing fire. As the flames were extinguished, thick black smoke filled the air.

There was a flurry of activity as the chief firefighter waved the ambulance over. It drove through the gate into the square itself and parked behind one of the fire engines. The paramedics ran over with their stretcher and bags of equipment. Nikki just couldn't bear it; she knew they were about to bring Derek out. Paul came running over.

"Derek's alive, he's in a bad way but he's still with us. Luckily, he was downstairs in the store area when the strike happened," he shouted to make himself heard over the noise of the storm.

There were gasps of relief all round, but the mood was still sombre, Derek wasn't out of the woods yet.

"I want to go with him in the ambulance," said Nikki.

Paul stopped her again. "You can't go with Derek; they're going to be working on him all the way to the hospital. I'll get my car and we'll go together." He looked round at the group of men standing there. "You might as well let the rest of your team go home for now. There won't be anything to do for the next few days."

Nikki looked round at her devastated team. "I'll be in contact soon as soon as I know more about Derek's condition, I promise. In the meantime, go home to your families," she assured them, and without any further persuasion they started the trek back through the wind and rain towards their accommodation.

Paul walked back to Mike and Richard. "I'm going to take Nikki to the hospital…" he said before his voice broke Richard put his arm around his son.

"Paul, everything can be fixed. The unit can be rebuilt, the temple can too. Hopefully, they got to Derek in time. You go with Nikki. We'll take care of everything else for now. There's really nothing much more you can do."

Paul pulled back from his dad as Mike patted him on the back. "At least this happened before anybody had moved in," he said. Mike was always the glass half full man.

They all looked across to the unit, which was no longer on fire, but the fire fighters were still trying to make the building safe. The ambulance had now set off with its blue lights on and siren blaring. Inside, the paramedics were working hard to save Derek's life.

Paul grabbed Nikki's hand. "Come on, let's get the car and go," he shouted in her ear.

They walked back through the driving rain. Paul could hardly bear to look at his collapsed Folly as they walked past the lake.

A short while later they were on their way and Nikki retrieved her phone from her pocket dreading the call she was about to make. She put it on speaker. The line was crackling but the call connected.

"Hi, Sue, it's Nikki. I'm sorry but Derek has been in an accident here at the Folly. He was working in a building that was struck by lightning—" Paul winced as he could hear Derek's wife's distressed cry. "He's still alive and is being ambulanced to the hospital. We're on our way there now. Yes, OK, see you soon." Nikki ended the call with a heavy sigh. "That was a horrible call to make, poor Sue. She's been a surrogate mother to me since Mum died."

There was a lot of surface water on the lanes and branches were falling from the trees making the drive treacherous. Paul drove his car slowly, glad that he had a four by four.

Nikki screamed. "Paul! Watch out! That tree's going to land on top of us!"

Paul quickly turned the steering wheel, moving the car sharply to the other side of the road grateful that nothing was coming towards him. The branches of the falling tree still brushed against the car. He pulled up with the hazard lights on and the driver of the truck that had been behind them dashed over. Between the two of them and despite the driving rain they managed to move the tree to the side of the road. Traffic had now stopped in both directions. Someone else came over and helped to pick up the branches that were lying in the road. As Paul pulled the branch that was lodged against the side of his car, he grimaced as he saw the dent and scratches it had caused.

After that, it was stop start all the way dodging branches and other debris until they got onto a major road. Paul and Nikki were silent lost in their own thoughts, appalled at the destruction caused by the storm and praying that Derek wouldn't die.

When they finally reached the hospital they made their way to the waiting room, it was too soon for any news about Derek. Five minutes later Sue and her daughter Lena turned up with red-rimmed eyes and panic all over their faces. They went over to speak to the reception then returned. Nikki stood up to give them big bear hugs.

"So, what happened?" asked Sue.

"Derek was working in one of the larger units in the artisan square when it was struck by lightning. Thankfully, he was downstairs in the storeroom at the time," said Paul. "We haven't been told about the extent of his injuries just yet."

Everyone sat in silence on the uncomfortable waiting room chairs. Nikki was sure she had read the posters on the wall at least a dozen times before the doctor eventually walked in.

"Mrs Sturgess?" he asked as Sue jumped up looking scared and anxious. "I'm Doctor Evans."

"This is our daughter Lena and Derek's bosses Nikki and Paul," said Sue, her voice trembling.

The doctor motioned to them all to sit down and he took the seat next to Sue.

"Derek has broken his collar bone and his right arm where a wooden beam fell on top of him. He has lacerations to his hands and face from broken glass and he has been intubated to treat the smoke inhalation," said the doctor.

"Will he be OK?" asked Lena whose face was blotchy and red from crying. She was terrified her dad was going to die.

The doctor looked sympathetically at the two crying women. "We're concerned about his lungs, but although it is too early to say for sure, I am hopeful that Derek will recover. You can go up to see him but obviously he won't be able to speak yet."

Nikki and Paul stood up relieved that Derek hadn't succumbed to his injuries. Now that they had been given the news Nikki started to cry, she had been trying to stay strong for Sue and Lena.

"We'll head off now," said Paul. His mind was racing with everything that had happened but at least Derek hadn't lost his life. "But if you need anything call either of us at any time day or night." Nikki nodded in agreement.

"Thank you both for coming to the hospital," Sue replied gratefully. "I'll keep you up to speed with Derek's progress."

Nikki gave her a final hug before the two women left with the doctor to go up to the ward.

The weather had calmed down significantly when they left the hospital and the drive back to the Folly was a lot easier. As they drove up they could see that the emergency vehicles had all left the property only to have been replaced by media vans. Paul groaned.

"That's all I need at the moment," he said tersely

As soon as Nikki and Paul got out of the car, two reporters ran up to them. "Mr Archer, is there any news on the chap who was inside the building?"

Just before Paul could answer Mike and Richard joined them. They could see Paul's pale face and the toll that today's events had taken on him and wanted to support him.

"Derek Sturgess has sustained broken bones and cuts and is currently on a ventilator being treated for smoke inhalation. The doctor is hopeful that Derek will recover, but he's still very poorly. He was undoubtedly saved by being downstairs at the time of the lightning strike," Paul said to the waiting reporters.

Mike spoke up next. "Obviously, there is quite a lot of structural damage both here in the square and to the actual Folly itself, but we will rebuild. Of course, it is obvious that our primary concern is for Derek's wellbeing, and we ask that you respect his family and leave them be while he recovers in hospital."

Richard leaned in close to Paul and Nikki. They could smell the smoke clinging to his clothes. "Why don't you get yourself back to the house for now and we'll have a look at everything first thing in the morning," he said.

Paul nodded; he had had quite enough for one day. They got back into the car and drove back round to Paul's house. The power was back on, and Cleo had thoughtfully left a lasagne for them to heat up. Neither of them slept properly that night, Nikki woke up at five the next morning to find that Paul's side of the bed was empty. She found him downstairs in the kitchen nursing a strong cup of coffee. He was very pale with black rings under his eyes. She walked up to him and wrapped her arms around his shoulders pulling him in close and they sat like that until Paul's coffee had gone cold.

"Come on, let's get ready to face the day and have some breakfast and hot coffee," said Nikki. "We've got a lot to do today."

Paul shook his head. "I honestly couldn't eat a thing right now, but a coffee would be good."

Nikki made some toast and was relieved to see Paul absentmindedly pick up a slice.

An hour later Mike, Richard and Tom knocked at the door.

"Ready to come and survey the damage mate?" Mike asked as Paul tugged on a pair of boots.

"I guess so," he replied, his shoulders were slumped, and he kept his face down.

Nikki jumped up too and they all took a slow walk down towards the folly. Although it was overcast, the wind had died right down, and it had stopped raining. Fortunately, the art castle had not suffered any damage. As they reached the lake the sight of the temple which had folded like a deck of cards was testament to the strength and power of the wind yesterday. Paul and Mike walked up to a small boat shed and pulled out a dinghy. There was only room for two, so Nikki waited with Richard and Tom.

"Actually, I think we might be in luck," said Mike as they reached the edge of the island. "Nothing is too badly broken. Sure, there are chips and cracks here and there, but I think they can be repaired. We'll need to fish the other two columns out of the lake."

Paul nodded in agreement. "Yes, we've definitely been lucky here. We can get the builders back in and hopefully they can put something in place to stop this happening again," he said.

"It was a freak storm," replied Mike. "It caused damage over half of the south of England. The temple was a sitting target unfortunately."

Having produced a plan of action for the folly they rowed back and put the dinghy away again.

Paul took Nikki's hand as they walked down towards the artisan square. He knew that she would find the scene distressing.

The sight before them was not good. The blackened shell of the unit and the filthy water in the square would obviously require a lot of work to put right again. There was smoke damage to the adjoining unit too.

"My inclination would be to demolish this unit and build it from scratch again," said Mike. The others nodded in agreement.

"I've got someone from the insurance company coming over later on this morning," said Tom as he checked his phone. "They should agree to the rebuild, it seems to be the obvious solution."

"We can also call in a firm that specialises in clean-up operations after an event like this. They should be able to sort out the smoke damage," said Mike. He was naturally very good at problem solving. He also hated seeing Paul looking so broken. Coming up with a good plan of action would re-energise him.

"How long do you think it would take to get things back to where they were?" asked Nikki wringing her hands. The enormity of the task in front of them was obvious.

"We were hoping to open up in July, but we will have to push that back by at least eight weeks," Richard replied.

"I'm more than happy to provide a financial incentive to get the work done as soon as possible," said Paul, who had cheered up a bit now that they were formulating a plan of action.

"I'll get four of my team back to continue working on the castle," said Nikki, glad that she could contribute to the more positive discussion. "And next week the rest can finish off the interiors here in the square."

Everyone nodded at Nikki's plan. They needed to keep the project moving.

This past week had been an absolute nightmare for Paul, but as Mike had pointed out, everything could be fixed with a little time. This had been the most harrowing few days of his life, and was most grateful for Nikki agreeing to give him a second chance. He wouldn't let anything come between them again.

CHAPTER EIGHT

Once the insurance company had given the go ahead to demolish and rebuild the unit in the artisan square, work had started up right away. The temple had been repaired quickly as the columns had only needed to be put firmly back into position with some small repairs to the chipped marble. The clean-up company had done an excellent job in repairing the smoke damage and clearing away all the mess from the square. By the beginning of the following week the work was all underway again. Paul was able to relax and was now busy collaborating remotely with the writers in America to adapt one of his novels into a screenplay. Nikki took advantage of the downtime to finish her sketches in readiness for painting the folly. The weather had been miserable and overcast for a few days but then the sun had returned, and Nikki had decided that today was the day to paint. She carried her easel down to her favourite spot at the edge of the lake and started to work. It was so therapeutic, Nikki loved to paint and was oblivious to the world around her as she concentrated.

"Hello, Nikki," said Ava which made her jump out of her skin.

"Hi, Ava, Riley and Cleo." Nikki smiled at them.

"I hope you don't mind us interrupting," said Cleo, admiring what Nikki had painted so far. "Wow, this painting is amazing!"

"Thank you, and of course I don't mind you interrupting," replied Nikki.

Nikki had well and truly been welcomed into the Archer family and was honoured to have been added to their WhatsApp group. She had developed a close friendship with Cleo, and she loved the children.

"Can I paint too?" Ava jumped up and down eagerly.

"No, Ava, Nikki's busy," said Cleo and Ava stuck out her bottom lip with tears filling her eyes.

Nikki looked at Ava's disappointed face and had an idea. "I'm busy today, but if it's OK with your mummy would you like to join me tomorrow and then you can paint? Try to wear something not quite so pretty as that dress you're wearing."

Ava twirled round to show off her new dress which for once wasn't pink. Cleo had been incredibly surprised and faintly relieved that her daughter had chosen a yellow dress when they had been shopping.

"If you don't mind Nikki then that would be fine by me,"

said Cleo. "Thank you, and it would free me up to take Riley to get his hair cut."

Nikki nodded. When Cleo had taken Riley to the barbershop before he had screamed the place down. "I take it that some bribery might be taking place to facilitate said haircut?" Nikki laughed.

"Yup, you've got it in one."

The next day Nikki left her own painting at the cottage and walked down to set up some paints with some fresh paper ready for Ava to use. She walked back up to collect Ava who today had dressed into some old pink dungarees which were now too short for her. Perfect for painting in. She was dancing round excitedly looking forward to her time with Nikki.

"Come on, let's go," she ordered, pulling Nikki along.

"Have fun," said Cleo as she put Riley into his car seat.

"Is there anything in particular you would like to paint today?" asked Nikki as they reached the easel. Ava looked thoughtful for a minute. "I want to paint the same picture as you," she replied, picking up a paintbrush.

Over the next two hours Nikki coached Ava as she carefully painted her interpretation of the temple. She was too small to be able to use an easel, but Nikki had adapted a tray for Ava to lean on as she painted. She was a budding artist thought Nikki and Cleo agreed when she returned from her successful mission with a short-haired Riley.

"Ava, that's really good." She admired her daughter's work.

"Was it harrowing at the barbers?" asked Nikki.

"Strangely, no," replied Cleo with a relieved smile on her face. "It's amazing what a brand-new unopened box of Lego can achieve."

"Well done you," said Nikki impressed with Cleo's ingenuity.

Later that evening she cooked a pasta bake while Paul finished a conference call to the writers in California. She poured them both a glass of wine and was just dishing up as Paul walked into the kitchen and put his arms around her.

"That smells great, I'm starving," he announced.

"Really?" Nikki laughed. "You put away a huge plate of sandwiches at lunchtime, not to mention the chocolate bars."

Paul kissed her. "I'm being nagged by my favourite girl."

"Too right," Nikki said as she kissed him back.

After dinner they sat outside enjoying the lovely warm evening.

"Nikki, why don't you move in with me?" Paul asked suddenly. "It would make sense, you're here most nights anyway."

Nikki's eyes shone with pleasure. "If you're sure it's not too soon, I would love to," she replied.

"I don't see any point in waiting besides, I like you cooking my dinner for me every night," Paul replied with a cheeky grin as Nikki gave him a shove.

"Well tomorrow morning I'm picking Dad up so that he can come and see the folly for the very first time," said Nikki. "I could collect the rest of my stuff from his house then. So, the day after?"

Paul stood up and pulled Nikki up with him. "There's no time like the present," he said.

"But it's getting late," Nikki replied.

"How long would it take to bring all your stuff over from the cottage? You can't have too much there surely?"

"Well, not too long with both of us," said Nikki, excited by this sudden turn of events.

"Let's get cracking then. At least you'll be partly moved in by tomorrow." Paul grabbed her hand and led her to the door.

Just an hour later and Nikki was hanging her clothes up in the wardrobe Paul had cleared for her. She felt so happy, never expecting the day to end like this.

Paul walked in with a bag holding Nikki's shoes and laughed as she threw herself into his arms. "I love you, Paul Archer," she said covering his face with kisses.

"I love you too, baby."

The next morning Nikki set off to pick her father up. The plan was to give him the full tour of the folly and then Richard and Janet had very kindly invited them all to lunch. She sang along to the radio, life was wonderful, she had never felt so happy.

Chris looked very smart in his cream chinos and white short-sleeved shirt; he was excited about his day out. The arthritis restricted his mobility which saddened him as he had always been a very active person. However, when the weather was warm like today the pain wasn't quite so bad. He was very keen to see the work that his team had been conducting at the folly.

"So, Dad, I've got something to tell you," said Nikki, fiddling about with her ponytail.

"What's that then, love?" he asked.

"Well, I've moved out of the cottage and in with Paul," she replied, anticipating her dad's answer.

Chris pulled a face. "Isn't it a bit too soon? It wasn't that long ago that he was round my house begging for your forgiveness."

"I know, Dad, I did wonder that myself. But we're so good together and I love him. We both know that life's too short not to take a few chances now and then."

Chris nodded sadly he still missed his wife even after all these years. "Well, it's your decision love, you're a big girl now," he said.

"Thanks Dad," Nikki replied, happy that the conversation hadn't been too laboured.

Chris looked impressed as Nikki drove through the gates

and parked outside the front of the house. "Very nice."

"It's all family here," said Nikki. "Paul's parent's, brother and cousin all live in these houses."

Chris felt sad then. He truly envied close families. Nikki was the only one of his three children who ever spent time with him. His daughter Jessica was very materialistic and was living with her wealthy boyfriend. His son Stuart was a very insular person and was living up in the north of England. He hadn't heard from him in over a year now apart from an impersonal birthday card.

"They're all lovely people," said Nikki as Paul walked out of the front door to greet them both.

"Hi, Chris, ready for the big tour?" Chris nodded; he was prepared to let bygones be bygones. If Paul made his daughter happy, then that was good enough for him.

They walked slowly back towards the gate; Nikki very mindful of her dad's pain levels.

"My pain isn't too bad at all today," said Chris as if he had read her mind.

He sat down in the front of the golf buggy and Nikki was happy to sit in the back while Paul drove them round for the tour. Chris's eyes opened in amazement when he saw the art castle, and like Nikki, he had laughed at the statue in the garden.

"I'm going to teach some art classes here," said Nikki. "As

long as it fits in around our work. I'm extremely excited about it."

Chris knew what a big sacrifice Nikki had made leaving her teaching job to help him with his work and he was incredibly happy that this opportunity had come along for his daughter. As they got back into the buggy to continue with the tour he put his arm on Paul's hand to stop him from driving off again.

"I'm so pleased to hear that you've got the chance to teach again love and I don't want you to feel tied to the decorating," he said.

"But I don't mind—" Nikki said.

"Well, the thing is, Matt has put his cards on the table and said that he would like to buy the decorating company. I know I won't be able to work anymore and it's certainly not fair on you to keep it going. How would you feel if I sold it to him, it would work for me and it sounds like it would be good for you too?"

Nikki tipped her head to one side as she thought about what her dad had just said. She didn't want her dad to sell his company just to free her up, but she was excited at the prospect of teaching art again.

Paul spoke first. "It sounds like a great solution to me."

Finally, Nikki nodded in agreement. "If that's what you want to do, Dad, then it's fine by me."

"Then it's settled, I'll call Matt later on to give him the good news," said Chris, relieved that Nikki was agreeable to his selling the company to Matt.

Just as Nikki had predicted, Chris loved the tranquillity of the lake and he chuckled at the temple on the island. He liked the quirkiness of the writer's cottages and was extremely impressed with the artisan square.

"You've got some imagination son, I'll give you that," he said to Paul when they drove back to the house.

"Thanks, Chris, I just hope it gives a lot of pleasure to the people who will be staying and working here," Paul replied.

They walked round to the back of Paul's parent's house and found them sitting out in the garden. As they stood up to greet Paul, Nikki and Chris, Janet gave a cry of surprise.

"Chris! It's been a long time!" she said.

Chris looked amazed and then gave a broad grin. "Janet and Richie! I never connected the Archer name with you two. What a lovely surprise."

Richard shook Chris's hand, obviously extremely excited to meet him.

"How do you all know each other?" asked Paul, surprised as this turn of events.

"Well, please sit down first," said Janet, who already knew from her conversations with Nikki that it would be painful for Chris to stand up for too long.

Once Richard had given Chris and Paul a bottle of lager

and Nikki a fruit juice as she was driving they started to reminisce.

"Well, right at the beginning when Janet and I had started seeing each other, I was in the same ten pin bowling team as Chris," said Richard.

"What was it called again?" asked Chris, trying to remember.

"It was the Bowlarks." Richard laughed. "We thought it was a clever play on words at the time."

"That's right, I remember now." Chris joined in with the laughter.

"I've never been able to bowl," said Janet. "But I used to go along to support them all with the other girlfriends. I used to have such a laugh with your girlfriend Stella."

"That was my mum," said Nikki, astounded at what she was hearing.

Janet looked at Nikki and smiled. "Your mum was a lovely lady; we were really close friends back in the day."

"Didn't you move to Canada?" asked Chris.

Richard nodded. "I had the job offer of a lifetime and so we decided that I should take it. We left about a week after we got married. You came to our wedding didn't you?"

"We did!" replied Chris.

"Of course, once we moved to Canada we tended to lose touch with all our friends here in the UK. There was no internet or social media back in those days," said Janet sadly.

"But I have very fond memories of the four of us having a lot of fun before that."

"This is incredible," said Paul. "I might have to put a twist like that into one of my novels, although of course one of you would have to be the villain of the piece."

Everybody enjoyed the afternoon. There were a lot of funny stories about things that Paul and Nikki's parents had all got up to when they were younger. Nikki hadn't seen her dad smile and laugh like that for such a long time. She realised that this was the first time he had been able to talk about her mum in such a positive and happy way and it was obviously doing him the world of good.

As Nikki stood up ready to drive her dad back home again, Janet spoke. "Chris, you must come over again soon. We've built up such a nice social life here now. We're in a quiz team that meets every Wednesday night at the pub. There are curry nights and we've even learned to play poker. It would be great if you could join us."

"I second that" said Richard. "You would fit in very nicely with our friends."

Chris nodded with a huge grin on his face. "You had me at curry night. It would be really good to meet people and make some new friends."

Nikki felt guilty. Chris hadn't socialised very much at all

over the past few years. He did go to the pub occasionally with Derek and Sue for Sunday lunch but the rest of the time he was stuck at home either watching tv or reading the newspaper. She didn't even know that he liked curry all that much. Well, that could be rectified straight away.

"Tell you what, Dad, let's get an Indian takeaway on the way home," she said. "Paul, you'll have to cook for yourself tonight."

Paul pretended to look hurt. "But I like it when you cook for me. Mum, maybe I could join you for dinner tonight," he whined.

Janet laughed. "You've got your work cut out with my son I'm afraid Nikki."

Don't I know it," Nikki replied as they started to walk off.

On the drive home Chris talked excitedly about meeting Janet and Richard again after so many years. Nikki couldn't remember the last time she'd seen him so animated. Perhaps she could persuade him to sell the family home and move closer once Matt had bought the business. She would dearly love to see her dad make new friends and have as good a retirement as possible.

Life was looking good all round in Nikki's eyes.

CHAPTER NINE

A few weeks later with the rebuilding work complete and all the electricity and water connected again, Nikki and Matt were able to get into the new unit to decorate it. The kitchen and bathroom fitters had worked quickly to install everything too.

"So, Matt, what are you going to call the company once you buy it?" asked Nikki as they painted the walls with the same lovely creamy colour as the other units.

Matt was buying the company from Chris once the folly project was complete. Paul's brother Tom had kindly drawn up the agreement passing ownership of contracts, equipment, and vans over to Matt.

"I couldn't come up with anything catchy like the chip shop called "New Cod on the block or the hairdressers called Fly-Away Hair." He laughed.

"Do you remember that builders van we saw one day that said, "Why go to the cowboys when the sheriff's in town?" asked Nikki. They both laughed at the memory.

"So, it's just going to be called Matteo Silva Decorating."

"I keep forgetting your dad's Spanish until I see your name written down," remarked Nikki. "We're really happy that you're buying the business and keeping most of the team on."

"Sadly I'll be losing Derek's experience," said Matt.

Derek had now been discharged from the hospital and was at home recovering from his broken bones and damaged lungs. When Nikki and Chris had gone to visit him a couple of days ago his voice was so sore and hoarse from the smoke inhalation had they told him not to speak too much. The brush with death however and the fact that Chris was selling the company had prompted him to retire too which Sue was more than happy about.

"I'm so excited about teaching art again," said Nikki. "It'll be all age groups too not just college students. Plus, I've got my art exhibition in Cambridge. That will be the first time I've ever displayed my work for everyone to see and potentially purchase." She walked over to the other side of the room to pick up a new tub of paint.

"I'm sure you'll be very successful, and it couldn't have happened to a nicer lady." Matt stopped what he was doing for a minute and picking up his coffee. He waited for Nikki to pick her mug up too. "I've got some other news too." He flushed.

"Do tell."

"I proposed to Erica last night and she said yes," said Matt shyly.

"Congratulations! About time too." Nikki gave him a hug. She was so pleased for her friend. "How long have you two been together now?"

"Er, twelve years, but we were only fifteen when we started going out together," Matt replied.

"Well, I'm very happy for you both," said Nikki.

"Maybe you won't be too far behind us," Matt commented, and it was Nikki's turn to blush this time.

"It's very early days yet," she said, but deep inside she had a feeling that it wouldn't be twelve years before Paul proposed to her.

They had a busy weekend ahead of them. On Saturday there was going to be Ava's fifth birthday party followed by the christening of Amanda and Simon's daughter Phoebe on Sunday. On Wednesday evening Paul was busy working on his laptop and Nikki was creating lesson plans when Amanda called. She put the phone on speaker.

"Hi, Amanda, everything OK? I've got you on speaker, Paul's here too," she asked her friend.

"Hi, Amanda," Paul called out.

"Hi, both of you. Yes, all good. Everything's ready for Sunday. I just wanted to call you to let you know that Melissa and Harry's baby boy was born this morning."

Nikki didn't feel the cold clenching of her heart at the mention of the new baby. She was grateful that she felt better about it now.

"So, I'm guessing they've called him Edward," said Nikki. "Some of our arguments were about Harry's insistence on calling a son Edward. I was never too keen on the name to be honest."

"Um, no," said Amanda. "You wouldn't ever be able to guess the name."

Nikki was surprised at that. Harry had really gone on and on about choosing the name Edward if they had been blessed with a son.

"Go on then, let's have it," she said wondering what they had chosen to call the new baby.

"They've called him Zeus Zebedee, or Zeezee for short," said Amanda sounding embarrassed.

Paul burst out laughing. "For goodness sake! What is it with all these weird and wonderful names nowadays?"

"It's like the old Harry was abducted by aliens and replaced by someone else," said Nikki. "His new fashion choices were strange enough but calling his son Zeus Zebedee? What on earth happened to him?"

"Melissa's a social media influencer," began Amanda.

Nikki didn't use social media at all, it had never interested her.

"She's actually quite well-known. Her dad is Leo Franks, the lead singer of the eighties band Wolf. Giving a baby an unusual name is quite common nowadays for people in the spotlight, it gets a lot of publicity."

"Poor kid though," said Paul. "He's paying the price for Melissa's fame."

"I love my brother dearly," said Amanda. "But I agree with you, the name is ridiculous."

"Thanks for the warning, at least we can try not to laugh if they come to the christening on Sunday," said Nikki as they ended the call.

Paul and Nikki fell about laughing.

"Carol and Jim, Amanda and Harry's parents will be mortified," said Nikki

"I don't think anybody could take that name seriously," replied Paul.

On Saturday afternoon they wandered over to Mike and Cleo's house laden with presents for Ava's fifth birthday party. This was a family gathering. The day before Ava had had a joint party with her friend Susie at an indoor play area. She had loved distributing the party bags and had insisted on making some up for the family too.

Nikki was thrilled because Chris had been included in the invitation. He had become a frequent visitor as Janet and Richard had introduced him to their social circle. Chris thrived from making new friends and he was finally starting to move on with his life instead of being in a permanent state of limbo since the death of his wife Stella sixteen years ago.

Ava was proudly driving Riley around the garden in her new pink battery-operated convertible. Riley couldn't stop laughing, enjoying himself immensely sitting in the passenger seat. Her eyes opened wide as she saw the birthday presents piling up on the table on the patio and she jumped out of the car excitedly and ran across to study them. Riley was trying to clamber over into the vacated driving seat, but Mike dashed up to collect him, his son was too little to try and drive the car. He started to scream, and he was hitting Mike as he was carried back towards the gathering. Janet tried to take him, but his tantrum was in full flow now.

Chris picked up a parcel and stood up. "Riley, I have something here for you." He waved it in front of the little boy.

Almost at once the tantrum was over, and Riley gave Chris a toothy grin as he stretched over to take the present from him.

Ava crossed her arms and pouted. "Why are you giving Riley a present? It's *my* birthday." "Ava! Don't be so rude," snapped Cleo.

"When Nikki was a little girl, her younger brother and sister used to cry when it was her birthday because they didn't understand why they weren't getting any presents too. So, we always bought them a small gift. Riley is too little to understand," said Chris, looking towards Cleo and Mike.

"I hope that was OK with you?" he said hoping that he hadn't overstretched the mark.

"Of course, it is," replied Mike. "That was very thoughtful of you."

As Riley eagerly opened his parcel to find a toy fire engine, Ava calmed down as she was handed her first present to open. Finally, it was time for her to open her presents from Nikki and Paul and clapped her hands with delight when she saw she had been given a child's size easel, a smock, paper, paints, and brushes.

"Thank you," she said excitedly. "Now I can put my easel next to yours Nikki."

Nikki smiled. "That's the general idea," she replied, happy that Ava was so pleased with her presents.

While everybody was eating. Paul's phone rang. He picked it up from the table in front of him, it was from an unknown number.

"Hello." His face went red, and he scowled. He walked away but Nikki could still hear him. "What do you want? I told you to never contact me again!" He stopped again. "No, you can't, I'm too busy. There's nothing that you can show me or tell me that would make me want to see you." Paul ended the call and threw his phone onto the grass.

Nikki jumped up, frowning. "What was that all about?"

"Bloody Valentina! That's what." Paul shook his head angrily as Janet signalled for him to watch his language in front of the children.

Nikki picked up Paul's phone, pleased to see that it wasn't damaged in any way. She felt relieved as Richard and Janet took the children back to the pink convertible as soon as it was obvious that Paul was worked up about something.

They sat back down in their seats.

"What's that all about, mate?" asked Mike.

"Valentina wanted to see me straight away as she had "something important" to tell me," said Paul, using air quotes. "Honestly, the cheek of the woman, I have absolutely nothing I want to say to her, I never want to see her again."

"Did she give you any indication of what she wanted to tell you?" asked Nikki, a nervous griping pain starting up in her stomach.

"Something life-changing apparently," Paul said. "Hopefully she got the message and will leave me alone now. Perhaps she thought I would take her back with open arms."

He turned to Nikki. "I'm going to go back to the house, I don't want to bring the mood down at Ava's party."

Nikki stood up. "It's OK, Dad and I will come with you, we've been here for long enough anyway."

Chris was spending the night with Nikki and Paul as he was going with them to the christening the next day. They said goodbye to everybody and made their way back to Paul's house.

Once they had gone Janet exhaled. "Why has Valentina come crawling back out of the woodwork after all this time?" She furrowed her brow. "I hope she leaves Paul alone now, he made it quite clear he wanted nothing to do with her."

Cleo nodded in agreement. "I hope so too. I don't want it to affect Nikki either."

Paul was in a quiet mood for the rest of the evening and thankfully Valentina didn't try to call or message him. Nikki was also hoping that it was just a one-off attempt to make contact again.

The next day they set off to the village where the christening was taking place.

"I wonder if Zeus Zebedee will make an appearance today," said Nikki causing Chris to shake his head in wonderment.

"Stupid name if you ask me, absolutely ridiculous," he said.

Chris's phone rang then. "Oh, it's the estate agent. I asked them to come round and value the house on Friday. I rather fancy moving closer to you all now," he said happily.

Nikki and Paul smiled at each other as Chris took the call. It would be lovely if he could live close by. He was enjoying his new lease of life with Janet, Richard and their friends and it would give Nikki peace of mind to be able to check in on her dad more often.

When Chris ended the call he shook his head. He couldn't believe what he had just heard.

"The estate agent said that he had a buyer for my house without it even going on the market. He has a family on his books who want to buy my house because it's in the catchment area for the school they want their children to attend."

"Wow, how convenient for you," said Nikki. "Now you won't have to worry about having lots of viewings."

"Well, there's a bit of a snag," said Chris. "They need to move in by the beginning of September. That's just a month away. There's no guarantee I will find somewhere myself by then."

"You can always stay with us," said Paul. "We've got loads of room, you're more than welcome." The prospect of Chris staying with them for a while didn't bother him at all. Like Nikki, he was pleased with the upturn in Chris's life.

Nikki smiled gratefully at Paul. She would have liked to have made that offer herself but although she was now officially living with Paul, she still felt that it was his house, and it wasn't a decision she felt able to make on her own.

"Thanks, Paul, that's really kind of you. But you've just started out together, you don't want an old man cramping your style," replied Chris. He really didn't want to get in the way.

"Honestly, it's fine. The opening of the folly site is only a month away and we'll both be busy getting that up and running. You wouldn't bother us at all, I promise. Call the agent back and accept their offer."

"Thank you both," said Chris, his voice breaking ever so slightly. "I've been offered a small fortune to sell the house, so I'd be mad not to I suppose."

"Definitely," said Nikki. "This is such a convenient option for you."

Chris returned the call and just a few minutes later everything was arranged.

"Looks like you have a house guest then. Tomorrow I'll organise a storage unit for all my stuff to go in the meantime. Thank you both," he said feeling relieved that such a quick and easy solution had presented itself.

"No, problem at all, Chris," Paul replied.

"Paul, Cleo once mentioned that Mike had a sister called Paris, but I've never heard any of you speak about her. Is she still with us?" asked Nikki.

Paul looked gave a heavy sigh and shook his head. "Ah, Paris. Well, as you probably know, when my uncle and aunt died, Mike and Paris came to live with us. We were all close.

Paris is just a year younger than Mike and me. Growing up she was a real tomboy and a lot of fun. She was also very sporty and popular at school and all the boys fancied her."

"So, what happened next?" asked Nikki.

"Well, when she was seventeen she met a lad who called himself Buster who was a couple of years older. She started to spend all her time with him. None of us liked him, he didn't go to college or have a job and Paris made no attempt to properly introduce him to the family. We started to notice the smell of cannabis whenever she came home. She was incredibly rude to Mum and Dad and really upset them by saying that they weren't her parents."

"How cruel," said Nikki and Paul nodded in agreement.

"Then she left home, and nobody saw her for about three years. One Christmas morning she turned up and we were all so shocked. Paris was twenty-one then, but she looked like a woman in her forties. Her hair was matted, there were black rings round her eyes, and she had scabs on the backs of her hands. Paris had always been slim, but by then she looked anorexic. Ruth, who was studying medicine at university asked her outright if she was using heroin and she nodded," said Paul remembering that day. Everyone had felt so sad at the state Paris had got herself into.

"That's terrible," said Chris.

"Was Buster with her?" asked Nikki.

"No, she came alone, and stayed for two or three days. Tom got up early one morning to go for a run and he caught Paris going through Mum's purse and, when he challenged her he discovered that she had taken some of Mum's jewellery and put it into her backpack. She had also taken a camera and some other bits and pieces of value. Everyone came rushing downstairs when they heard the commotion and then the doorbell rang, Buster was waiting for her," said Paul.

"Paris had only turned up to steal from you then?" asked Nikki her mouth opened in shock at this story and imagining how heart-broken the whole family must have felt.

"Yep," Paul replied. "Paris had made all the right noises when Ruth had suggested some rehab options for her, but she obviously didn't have any intention of going. Suffice to say we haven't seen her for ten years now. For all we know she died of her addiction. If she's still alive, I sincerely hope that she sorted herself out."

Nikki and Chris both nodded. What more could they say?

The christening was a lovely occasion and Nikki was honoured to be one of the godmothers for little Phoebe who was as good as gold throughout the service.

Harry, Melissa, and Zeus Zebedee didn't turn up in the end, they were settling down into a new routine as the baby wasn't even a week old. Having spoken to Amanda's parents Nikki got the distinct impression that they were quite embarrassed about the unusual name and were relieved that they hadn't turned up at the christening.

It was early evening when Paul, Nikki and Chris arrived back home. Richard was at the front of his house washing his car and he waved them over.

"How was your day? Do you fancy joining us for drinks?" he asked cordially.

They wandered over to the house and Janet produced a bottle of wine for her to share with Nikki while Richard, Paul and Chris settled for lagers.

"Dad's had some exciting news today," said Nikki, who was thrilled that her dad would be moving closer to them.

"What's happened, Chris?" asked Richard.

"I've somehow managed to sell my house without it going onto the market. The snag is that the family want to move in by the start of September. It's unlikely I'll find something else in that time, so Paul and Nikki have kindly offered to put me up. I want to buy something over this way, makes sense with my new social life thanks to you both and to be closer to Nikki of course."

Richard jumped up. "We have a bungalow sitting empty next door. Why don't you move in there? It makes perfect sense to me."

Paul and Nikki nodded. It hadn't even occurred to them to consider the bungalow as a place for Chris to live. All the properties were owned by the development company owned by Mike and Paul.

"It was built four years ago, and nobody has ever lived in it. Why not let Chris live there?" said Paul.

"It would be perfect for you, Dad, especially with your mobility, and you would close to us all," said Nikki smiling happily at this turn of events.

"Come on, let's show you round now," said Janet and they all trouped next door with Chris shaking his head. Everyone was being so kind.

Much like the houses, the bungalow was an open-plan space. It had three bedrooms and a small garden.

Chris was choked up and shaking his head like he was in a dream. "I can't believe all of this. A couple of months ago I was living on my own in a large rambling house with very little going on. Now, I've rediscovered old friends, made some new friends and you're offering to let me live in this wonderful bungalow. Thank you all so much. You're all exceedingly kind."

Janet hugged him. "Welcome to the neighbourhood."

CHAPTER TEN

On Monday morning, Nikki drove Chris home and made some phone calls relating to the sale of the house. She would have to spend a good couple of days helping Chris to declutter before the move. He had always kept Stella's clothes and belongings as he couldn't bear to part with anything she had owned.

Nikki had spoken gently to Chris. "I think it's time we let Mum go now, Dad. This is a fresh start for you, and she wouldn't want you to keep all her stuff. What would it achieve?"

Chris had broken down. It broke his heart to get rid of everything that had belonged to his beloved wife, but Nikki was right. This was a fresh start for him and the right time to let go of the past.

Nikki arrived home at lunchtime having promised to return at the end of the week to start the decluttering process. She needed to be at the art castle for the next two days as it was having a full safety inspection. Paul was sitting hard at work on his laptop, and she wrapped her arms around him and gave him a tender kiss.

"I'm so happy. I've got the best partner in the world, I live in a beautiful place, I'm going to teach art again and Dad is moving to the folly. Life is perfect," she said, her eyes filling with unexpected tears.

Paul smiled. "I would have to agree with you there. This film script adaptation is going well too. Trouble is, they want me to fly back out to the Los Angeles in the next week or so, but I've put them off until after the opening of the folly. That's much more important to me now."

"Absolutely," replied Nikki, walking towards the kitchen.

"At least you can still have your daily Zoom calls with the writers out there."

Paul's phone rang and straight away he could see that it was the same unknown number that Valentina had used on Saturday. He didn't take the call.

"What does the woman want with me? I've made it clear I don't want anything to do with her," he snapped. When he had last seen Valentina she had tried to deny everything he had discovered about the relationship she had been having with someone he had considered a friend. Finally, she had confessed but had never apologised for her actions. Paul had told her to never come anywhere near him again, it was over, and nothing would change his mind. After a few attempts to change his mind, Valentina had finally got the message. He certainly didn't want to start up a dialogue with her now.

Paul's whole demeanour had changed since the unsettling call he received from Valentina on Saturday. He wasn't his usual chatty self and had retreated into a world of his own. He had a lot on his plate now with the opening of the folly and the film adaptation work. Especially after all the stress that the storm damage had given him. This latest development could potentially be the final limit. Nikki took a cup of coffee over to him and spoke decisively.

"Let's just get this over with now," said Nikki. "Call Valentina back, put her on speaker and we'll find out exactly what it is she wants. Otherwise, this will just hang over us."

Paul sighed. "I honestly can't bear to speak to her. But I get what you're saying. OK, let's do it."

They sat side by side on the sofa and Paul called the number back. He put the speaker on.

"Paul, thank you for calling me," purred Valentina in a deep pleasant, accented voice.

"I'm only calling to find out what you want from me, I have a new partner now and she's sitting right here," said Paul, unable to keep the tension out of his voice.

"Oh." Valentina hadn't expected Paul to say that. "Then what I have to tell you will affect you both."

Paul raked his hair with his hands while Nikki clenched her hands so tightly together that she could feel her fingernails digging in.

"What on earth are you talking about?" Paul snapped. "You can't possibly say anything that would affect both myself and Nikki."

"Nikki," Valentina repeated slowly taking this information in. "Please, let me come to your house, what I have to tell you will make more sense to you then."

Paul looked at Nikki, who pulled a face and then nodded. "How soon can you be here?" he demanded.

"I will be there in one hour," she replied, and Nikki wondered if she had imagined the triumph in her voice.

They both paced nervously around the house wondering what amazing news Valentina wanted to convey to them both.

Soon the buzzer announced her arrival and Paul pressed the button to open the gates to allow Valentina to drive through. The doorbell rang a few minutes later and Paul stood still for a moment psyching himself up before walking slowly towards the front door.

Nikki waited in the kitchen, her stomach contracting nervously. Paul came back through a moment later followed by a tall slim beautiful woman wearing a bright red fitted dress showing off a figure any model would be proud of. She had a mane of long black glossy hair. She was pushing a buggy in front of her holding a sleeping little boy. Just for a moment Valentina stared right into Nikki's eyes with an air of extreme confidence.

Paul sat down heavily onto the sofa pulling Nikki down next to him. Valentina looked a bit unsure for a moment before sitting delicately down on the opposite sofa crossing her long shapely legs.

"So, what do you want from us, Valentina?" asked Paul. He didn't offer her a drink, he just wanted to hear her out and then send her packing hopefully forever this time.

She waved her hand towards the sleeping child. "This is my son Thiago; he is our son, Paul," she said.

Paul jumped straight up. "Don't you dare come here and lie to me!" he shouted which caused the child to stir. "I haven't seen you for almost two years, there is no way that this child is mine."

"Thiago is sixteen months old. I found out I was pregnant just after you asked me to leave," said Valentina.

"And why did I ask you to leave? Because you were having sex with another man throughout our relationship. Don't try and land this all at my feet. Have you visited him and been sent away? Thought you would try your luck with me?" raged Paul.

Paul paced with his fists clenched and a huge scowl on his face. Valentina remained perfectly calm throughout his outburst.

"Adam had a vasectomy after his wife had their third child. He didn't want any more children," she said calmly.

Nikki was disgusted at Valentina's fly away comment about the man she had had an affair with. She obviously didn't care about the wife and three children that she and Adam had betrayed.

"But you were on the pill, for goodness sake!" shouted Paul, causing the little boy to wake up and cry.

Valentina unstrapped him from his buggy and cradled him in her arms making soothing noises. "Paul, look at him and you will see. He has the same colour hair as you, your dimples—"

Nikki suddenly felt bile rise in her throat and her heart started to pound. She could see the likeness now that Valentina had pointed it out. Paul looked at the boy too and he was suddenly filled with doubt.

"So where did you go after we split up?" he asked.

"When I found out I was pregnant I went back home to Majorca. My parents were so angry with me, and ashamed that their daughter could have a child out of wedlock. They have never wanted to see their grandson and I have been living with my friend Maria. But Thiago needs to know his father now he is getting older. We just need somewhere to live." Valentina looked at Paul with a sheen of tears in her eyes.

"So, you want me to accept that this child is mine and buy you a house. Am I right?" asked Paul. "I want a DNA test carried out of course."

Thiago had stopped crying. Valentina walked over to Paul.

"Please, hold your son while I get some papers out of my bag. I knew you would ask for a DNA test," she said with confidence.

Paul awkwardly took the child from Valentina. Thiago had Valentina's dark eyes and they stared up at Paul. Then, he smiled, and Paul's heart melted. He smiled back at the little boy. Nikki felt her stomach clench and she broke out in a sweat. She stood up and walked through to the kitchen not wanting to make it obvious how the news about Thiago had affected her. Valentina looked incredibly pleased at this interaction between Paul and Thiago and the affect her arrival was clearly having on Nikki. She produced a form and a tube holding a swab.

"Please read everything here. You just need to fill out your details on the form and supply the swab sample, then we will both get the results in a few days' time," Valentina said, holding her arms out for Thiago while Paul took the paperwork from her.

He glanced across at Nikki before he completed the form and rolled the swab around his cheek before returning it all to

Valentina who had busied herself putting Thiago back into his buggy.

"I will post this," she said. "Once the results come back confirming that you are Thiago's father, we can discuss our living arrangements."

Paul had nothing more to say to Valentina and led her silently back to the front door. She tried to hug Paul be he jumped away from her. "Let me make myself perfectly clear," he said through clenched teeth.

"If Thiago is my son, I will of course want to spend time with him. But you mean nothing to me at all. I love Nikki, my future is with Nikki. Any future meetings between us will be very brief."

Valentina wasn't used to being spoken to like this, but she let the outburst go and glanced over to where Nikki was standing. "I understand," she whispered before leaving the house.

Paul shut the front door behind her and then leaned heavily against it. Nikki's heart went out to him. He walked towards her, and she held him tightly before bursting into tears. Paul was trembling. "I…I can't believe this," he said in utter disbelief. "I'm so sorry, Nikki."

"Don't you dare apologise," Nikki replied through her tears. "This has been a massive shock for us both."

Nikki pulled away from Paul and led him back to the sofa. "We're in this together. If Thiago is your son, we will adapt our lives accordingly. Paul, we're a team, we're stronger than anything Valentina can throw at us. Remember that. In the meantime, let's focus on the folly." She had sounded far braver than she felt, but she wanted to be strong for Paul.

"I wouldn't blame you if you wanted to walk away from this," Paul replied, and Nikki could see that his hands were trembling at the prospect of so much change.

"Nope! Not happening," said Nikki. "That's not an option." But deep down she wondered if she really could be strong enough to cope with Valentina and a child who could potentially be Paul's.

CHAPTER ELEVEN

The next morning Nikki and Paul met with Tom and Richard at the art castle. It was an exciting moment for them all as the building had now officially been signed off having passed all its health and safety inspections. Nikki had been tasked with ordering all the equipment needed for the large, light bright airy rooms. She had bought chairs, tables, and stools. There were easels, drawing equipment, paints and paper for the art rooms neatly stored away in lockable cupboards. She had bought a kiln, potter's wheels, clay, plaster, wax, and resins. The break room had smart navy-blue diner-style booths with a small but well-equipped white fitted kitchen.

"This looks fabulous, Nikki," said Richard. "Keeping the paintwork and walls all white definitely gives a feeling of light and space"

"Thanks, Richard." Nikki grinned. "It's important to have plenty of light for art. I'm really looking forward to teaching here."

They went upstairs where there were rooms for the guests signing up for residential courses. These had also been painted in white but with light oak wooden floors. They all had a comfortable king-size bed with navy-blue bedding which matched the curtains and the small double sofa. There was also a smart ensuite shower room.

Paul, who had been quiet since Valentina's visit the day before, smiled broadly. "This is actually happening! My dream is finally taking shape. I couldn't have achieved this without you guys."

"It's been demanding work," agreed Mike, who had had his doubts when Paul had initially broached the subject of the folly. "But once the entire site is open, it's going to be amazing."

They all trouped back downstairs to go outside.

"Have you come up with a timetable for the castle yet?" asked Richard.

Nikki nodded. "I've been in contact with the local schools and offered my support with the coursework. I have also placed a few local ads giving the details of some of the courses I would like to run. Hopefully we will get a good response."

The guys all looked impressed with what Nikki said.

"Sounds like you're going to be very busy," said Tom.

"I can't wait," said Nikki. "I've really missed teaching."

Mike led them round to the back of the castle. Next to the

garden was a new tarmacked car park.

"This is nicely hidden from the façade of the castle. We really needed to put this in so that we can avoid having schoolkids wandering around all over the place, especially in the winter months when it'll be wet and muddy. We've put in a picnic area at the end of the garden so that they can eat their packed lunches out there when the weather is good," he said.

Paul nodded, grateful that Mike had overseen the more practical elements of the folly. He would never have thought about parking or picnic areas.

"So, what's next in our schedule?" he asked.

"We have the safety inspection for the Tudor house and the cottages next week," said Richard, referring to his notes. "The artisan square and the diner will be inspected the week after that."

"Why didn't we get everything signed off at the same time?" asked Nikki.

"The inspectors point out some things that might need to be moved or changed to get it up to standard. I'm expecting a snagging list for the square as we have a lot of different requirements for each unit. We did well not to get anything questioned for the castle. I didn't want to overstretch anyone with extra work," replied Richard.

"Ah, I see, that makes perfect sense now," said Nikki, who had thoroughly enjoyed learning about project management.

"Did I see Valentina outside your house yesterday?" asked Tom.

Paul and Nikki both pulled faces. "Yes, she turned up with a little boy she is claiming to be mine," said Paul bitterly.

Richard, Tom and Mike couldn't believe what Paul had said and stared at him open mouthed. They all knew how devious Valentina had been in the past.

"You didn't believe her surely?" asked Richard.

"I carried out a swab sample for a DNA test," said Paul. "She claims she was already pregnant when I sent her packing and that he's definitely my child. There's an element of reasonable doubt as Thiago's hair and the dimples on his face do have some similarity to mine. We should find out at the end of the week if he is my son."

Mike looked at Nikki. "How are you coping with this bombshell Nikki?" he asked

Her chin wobbled and she took a deep breath to try and stop herself crying. "I'm here to support Paul all the way. If Thiago is his son then we'll deal with it together," she replied, her eyes bright with the unshed tears.

Paul put his arm around her and pulled her close. "I don't deserve you," he said, kissing her gently.

"We're all here for you son," said Richard, thinking that it would be strange to get used to having a grandson who didn't speak English.

Over the next few days, Nikki travelled over to Chris's house to help him to clear out her mother's belongings. They had donated clothing, shoes, bags, and ornaments to a local charity shop. Nikki had also made several runs to the local dump. Finally, Nikki decided to clear out the loft. She handed down a case to Chris which held a lot of family photos and documents.

"So, is there anything up in the loft you want to keep Dad?" she asked.

Chris was already engrossed in looking through the contents of the case. "I don't think so love. Just check in case there's anything you want to keep."

Nikki brought down the Christmas tree and decorations remembering how magical her mum had made the festive season for them all. After Stella had died Christmas had been a much more sombre affair.

Nikki saw a picture frame leaning against the wall at the back of the loft. Intrigued, she picked it up and turned it round to face her. It was a portrait of a serious-looking older gentleman sitting at a very grand desk. He had white hair and a matching beard with a pair of glasses sitting at the end of his nose. There was a large bookshelf behind him. Nikki guessed that this had been painted sometime during the nineteenth century. It needed a good clean as a lot of the detail was not immediately obvious to the eye. She took it downstairs.

"Dad, what do you know about this painting?" she asked.

Chris looked up and then started to laugh. "Years ago, when you were all young, your mother and I went to a jumble sale. As we wandered around I saw this painting, it reminded me of a photo of my great grandad…." Chris quickly picked up a pile of old photos and flicked through them. He pulled one out to show Nikki. "Here's a photo of him, Jim Pembroke. I thought they looked similar despite the obvious difference in social standing."

Nikki looked at the photo. It was of an older man with white hair, huge mutton chops and a beard. Jim Pembroke wore a white collarless shirt with a waistcoat. He was sitting at a table nursing a tankard smiling broadly. The man in the portrait stared straight out with a sombre face. However, in a good light Nikki could see why Chris had seen a similarity between the two men.

"Your mum hated the painting and was cross that I had bought it. It only cost me fifty pence. When we got it home she refused to let me put it up anywhere, so it ended up in the loft."

"May I have it, Dad?" asked Nikki. "I did some restoration work when I was at Uni, and I would love to have a go at cleaning this up."

"Feel free, love, I don't want him now. Perhaps you could try and find out who he is."

"Maybe. It'll have to go on the back burner for now as we have the opening of the folly coming up as well as all the drama with Valentina."

Chris shook his head. "I'm so sorry you have to go through all that hassle with that woman."

Nikki shrugged. "If Thiago is Paul's son, and I suspect he is then we'll just have to get on with our lives. We'll have to learn Spanish to help Paul to bond with him. Valentina speaks perfect English. Paul said that she came over to England when she was twenty to work as a translator and she ended up working for an international law firm. I guess that's where she got a taste of the good life mixing in those sorts of circles."

"She sounds horrible."

"Now you're moving over to the folly you'll see a lot more of her I guess. Although if Paul has his way the contact with her will be minimal. But we can't just expect her to leave Thiago with us for a weekend and go off, it would be too distressing for the child."

She was still coming to terms with the sudden change in the dynamic in her relationship with Paul. She knew he was also struggling with Valentina's news.

"You're such a lovely person, I'm so proud of you," said Chris. His daughter had always been so kind, it wouldn't be in her nature to turn her back on Paul.

"I take after my dad," replied Nikki giving him a big hug.

She loved him so much and couldn't understand why her brother and sister didn't want to spend any time with him.

"Now it's another trip to the dump for me, I need to get rid of all this Christmas stuff," she said as tears threatened at the prospect of discarding the memories. But now was the right time to make new memories, her mum would have understood.

"Do you want me to come with you?" asked Chris.

"No, it's fine. I'm going to head off home straight from there. I'll stay overnight on Monday so we can both be here for the removal men," said Nikki. It would be the end of an era to move out of this house, but she was so happy about her dad's change in luck, and it would be a lovely fresh start for him.

"OK, love, thanks for helping me with all this. I could never have managed on my own," replied Chris gratefully. Nikki kissed him. "I'm really pleased you're moving over to the folly; we can see each other every day."

Chris nodded in agreement. "I'm really looking forward to moving over there, as well as seeing you, I have a whole new life."

"I'm pleased for you, it's lovely you've reconnected with Janet and Richard. OK then, see you in a few days," replied Nikki as she left the house.

Chris closed the door behind his daughter. Both of their lives had changed in such a short space of time. He felt like he was the luckiest man in the world.

On Saturday morning a courier arrived with a package for Paul, it had the results of the DNA test.

"Nikki, the results have arrived," he called, and she ran down the stairs to join him.

They went out to the kitchen and Paul hastily handed the package to Nikki, his hands were shaking, and his breathing had become heavy. Nikki picked up a pair of scissors and slit the package open. A few leaflets about the DNA testing company dropped out and she was left with the piece of paper which had the potential to change both of their lives forever. She exhaled and scanned the information in the letter.

"Thiago's your son," Nikki said, before bursting into tears.

Paul hugged her tightly to him and he also sobbed. Nikki recovered first.

"OK, my love, this is us now and we'll make it work. Thiago is so little; he doesn't understand the change that's coming his way, we'll have to make the transition nice and easy for him," she said, knowing that they would have to be practical about what lay ahead of them.

Paul nodded reaching over to the side for a tissue before wiping his eyes. "I'm glad I have you to support me with this, I love you so much."

"I love you too. I'm guessing we can expect a call from Valentina sometime today."

Almost at once the buzzer sounded to let them know that somebody wanted to come in through the gate. Paul looked at the monitor.

"Well, here she is now. She certainly didn't give us any breathing space," he said quietly.

Soon Valentina pushing Thiago in his buggy turned up at the front door. She looked triumphantly at Nikki before she addressed Paul.

"You have also received the results today?" she asked.

"We did," replied Paul.

Nikki busied herself making a fresh pot of coffee. "Valentina would Thiago like some orange juice?"

Valentina nodded, hardly able to keep the beaming smile from her face. "Yes please. Wait, I have his cup here." She pulled a cup with a lid out of her bag, and she handed it to Nikki before sitting down really close to Paul. She acknowledged the coffee and juice that was handed over by Nikki and then turned to face Paul.

"Right," Paul said. "So firstly, are you planning to remain permanently here in the UK?"

Valentina nodded. "Yes, our son needs to know his father," she replied placing her hand on his knee causing Paul to flinch at her touch. He pushed her hand away before continuing.

"OK, I've been thinking about where you might live. The town is just a thirty-minute drive away and there are some nice new homes there. You'll be closer to more services than we are here and there's actually an international school in the town which might well give you some other Spanish speaking families to befriend potentially," said Paul.

"No!" said Valentina fervently. "That is too far away, we need to be much closer. Thiago is already confused about where we are now, it wouldn't be fair to him."

She looked around the huge kitchen and out into the large garden beyond.

"This is an enormous house, why can't we live here?" she asked, obviously thrilled that she had the upper hand in this new situation.

Paul jumped up and went to put his arm around Nikki who had looked very shocked at Valentina's suggestion.

"No, Valentina, that's absolutely out of the question. I don't want you here and besides, you mentioned Thiago getting confused by living a little bit further away, how confusing would it be for him to have both you and Nikki here?" he said firmly.

"So, this is the other thing I wanted to discuss," said Valentina. She was ready to play her trump card. "You are right, it would confuse our son to have both me and Nikki in the picture. Until he gets to know you properly, I must insist that Nikki stays out of his life." She glanced quickly at Nikki and saw that her announcement had had the desired effect.

Nikki was staring at her with wide eyes and her mouth opened looking shocked.

"Now you're being ridiculous!" Paul snapped. "You can't dictate what Nikki can and cannot do. She's my partner and Thiago will just have to learn that fact, sooner rather than later!"

Valentina stood up abruptly and prepared to leave. She flung her hair defiantly over her shoulder. "Paul, this is my final word on the matter. I want to live closer to you. OK, maybe not here, but how about the cottage at the gate? However, if you don't agree to Nikki staying away from us, I will book flights back to Majorca and you will never see your son again. You have until Sunday night to give me your answer!"

Without waiting for either Paul or Nikki to stand up she hurried to the door and left the house.

CHAPTER TWELVE

After Valentina had left, Paul paced — something Nikki had learned to recognise as his way to manage stress. "The evil, horrible, nasty cow!" he shouted. "She's like a wrecking ball, coming in here and dictating what should and shouldn't happen in my life! I can't believe she had the nerve—"

Nikki opened the patio doors and went to sit down outside, after a short while Paul joined her. He leaned over and clasped her hand.

"I'm so, so sorry you had to listen to that ...rubbish coming out of her mouth," he said.

Nikki sighed. "Well, playing devil's advocate, but Valentina does have a point. It would confuse Thiago to have a mum, dad and a Nikki." She burst into tears at that thought. She would never be anybody's mum.

Paul jumped up and hugged Nikki closely letting her tears

flow.

"There's no way that you're moving out just to please Valentina."

"You don't understand, this will be your only chance to be a dad if you stay with me. I couldn't take that chance away from you, even if it means that I have to move out."

Paul gaped at her. "What on earth are you talking about?"

Nikki sobbed. "Harry and I tried for years to have a baby, and look at him now, he is the proud father of Zeus Zebedee. It was clearly my fault that we couldn't have children."

Paul sighed and waited for Nikki to calm down. "Did the doctors ever tell you that you couldn't get pregnant?"

"Well, no, he couldn't find anything wrong with either of us." She sniffed.

"I'm a firm believer that things happen for a reason. Just because it didn't happen for you in the past, there's no reason it won't happen for you in the future." Gradually Nikki's breathing slowed down. "See? Valentina is already getting what she wants. You're upset and I'm feeling anxious. I don't want you to move out."

Nikki gave a heavy sigh. "OK, there are options I suppose. I can go shopping, visit Amanda, hang out with Dad, or give Ava some art lessons. If I'm in the house at the same time, I'll just keep out of the way. To start with anyway. I don't think we should let Valentina dictate to us for too long."

Paul sat and considered what Nikki had just said. "If you're happy with that initial arrangement, I'll agree to it, But I'll make it clear that you will only make yourself scarce in the short term. And another thing, I don't want her living here at the folly. She would make everybody's life a misery."

Nikki nodded. "I agree with you there. If she doesn't want to live in the town then perhaps we can find her somewhere to live in Honesty. That might be the best compromise we can produce. I'll stay away initially but she can't live here at the folly," she replied.

Paul picked up his phone. "I'll invite everyone round here so we can let them know what's going on. After all, Mum and Dad have just gained another grandson," he said still in a state of shock at the news.

Mike and Cleo at once responded asking everyone to go over to their house instead so that the children could play while the family chatted which made better sense. Once everyone was assembled Paul and Nikki went through everything they had discussed after Valentina had stormed out.

"Nikki, you're an absolute diamond," said Tom, giving her a hug. "This is a horrible situation for you to be in."

Nikki smiled. "Well, it's not great, but, hey, on a positive note, you're all gaining a new little nephew and grandchild."

Janet shook her head in disbelief. "I know you're telling me that I have a new grandson, but it feels so weird. But of course, we'll welcome him into the family with open arms. We'll try to learn a little Spanish too. Although I don't trust Valentina one jot."

"How do you feel about being a dad, Paul?" asked Cleo.

Paul shook his head. "It still doesn't feel real. I'm sure it will take some time for it to all sink in. But I didn't feel a rush of love for him once I knew I was his dad."

"Don't worry, It'll come. He's just an innocent child. We'll all learn to love him I'm sure of that." Janet nodded as if she was reassuring herself too.

Paul gave a wry smile. "Thanks for your support everyone. I'll call Valentina later and let her know what we have decided to do. In the meantime, we'll check out the property market down the road in Honesty."

Paul could feel Valentina gloating when he called her to say what they had decided to do. She baulked about not living at the folly at first but when she heard the firmness in Paul's voice she agreed to going to look at a cottage in Honesty he had seen online with him the following week.

"If you come on Tuesday morning at ten, I'll arrange a viewing for us," he said.

"Will Nikki be there?" asked Valentina.

"Not first thing no, she's spending Monday night in the town with her dad," he replied.

Paul didn't elaborate about the fact that Chris was moving

into the bungalow, which was nothing to do with Valentina.

"Very well, I'll see you first thing on Tuesday morning," she replied happily.

Paul pulled a face once the call ended.

"Is she happy with what you suggested?" asked Nikki.

"She didn't like the fact that I wasn't going to let her live here at the folly, but of course she's delighted that you'll be keeping out of the way to start with," Paul replied.

"I'm sure she was ecstatic about that point," said Nikki hating the way her life was about to change.

Paul nodded then stood up. "Let's get out of here tomorrow for the day, drive down to the coast perhaps," he said, desperate for a change of scenery.

"Sounds wonderful, leave the picnic to me," replied Nikki.

On Monday, as Nikki was preparing to leave to stay the night with Chris, Paul received a call from Tom. It was a brief call.

"Everything OK?" asked Nikki.

"Yes, Tom's just invited me to join the five a side football match tonight. He normally plays with some of the guys from the conference centre and one of them has had to drop out. Then afterwards we're going to the pub," Paul replied.

Nikki smiled. "That's wonderful. A night out with the boys will take your mind off everything." She kissed him. "See you tomorrow, love. I'm super excited that Dad is moving here tomorrow."

The next morning Valentina buzzed to come through the gates just after nine o'clock. She had left Thiago with a babysitter for the morning to allow her to have some proper time alone with Paul. The front door was open slightly and Paul called down from upstairs.

"Come in, Valentina, I'll be down in a minute."

Valentina smiled to herself as she wandered around the rooms, she was sure she could soon persuade Paul to give it another try with her. She scoffed to herself as she thought about Nikki. In her opinion, Nikki was nowhere as polished or sophisticated as she was. The woman didn't even appear to wear designer clothes, have a decent haircut and there was no evidence of fillers or Botox. Valentina knew that Paul had always admired her classiness. Yes, he would soon tire of dull old Nikki. She looked in the utility room and saw Paul's freshly ironed shirts hanging up. She would have to be destitute or desperate before she ever ironed a man's shirts. She looked down at her beautifully manicured nails. No, menial tasks didn't appeal to her at all. Some movement on the small screen in the kitchen caught her eye. It was the security camera, and she could see a red Mini driving up towards the house. This must be Nikki. An idea formed suddenly in her mind, but she would have to be quick.

Nikki let herself into the house, she had seen Valentina's car parked outside and at once felt the nervous griping pain in her stomach whenever she knew she was about to meet her.

"I'm home!" she called out as she walked through to the kitchen before stopping abruptly. Valentina was sitting at the breakfast bar dressed in nothing but one of Paul's white shirts. She smiled victoriously at Nikki before feigning surprise.

"Oh, I don't think Paul was expecting you back quite this early. He invited me round to talk things through last night. We started to reminisce about old times and well, here we are." She waved her hands across her body to emphasize the fact that she was wearing Paul's shirt.

Nikki crinkled up her face and she felt tears pricking at her eyelids. " Paul was going to play football with Tom last night," she said slowly. Her heart hammered so hard she was sure that Valentina could hear it. She sat down, her hands shaking.

Valentina laughed harshly. "That's what he told you yes, but in fact…" she tailed off. This couldn't have played out better for Valentina. If she could just get Nikki to leave everything would be perfect.

A moment later Paul, with his arm in a sling along with Tom, came down the stairs and walked out into the kitchen. They stopped and gaped at the scene in front of them.

Valentina looked slightly nervous now. She wasn't expecting to see Tom too. She had also wanted a bit more time to try and persuade Nikki that she was telling the truth and plant some seeds of doubt into her head.

"Valentina! What on earth is going on?" asked Paul scowling at her.

"Apparently you invited her round for a chat last night which led to a night of passion," said Nikki, realising that Paul was as surprised as she was to see Valentina wearing his shirt. "And what have you done to your arm?" She took in Paul's rough appearance and the sling he was wearing.

"Well, as Valentina knows, I didn't invite her round last night. Tom nipped downstairs and opened the front door when she buzzed in this morning. I managed to dislocate my shoulder last night playing football as well as knocking myself out. The doctor told Tom to stay and keep an eye on me. He had to help me to get dressed this morning. So, I am mystified as to why Valentina is pretending to have spent the night with me when I honestly can't bear being anywhere near her anymore," snapped Paul. Valentina was nothing but trouble.

Valentina sloped off and re-emerged fully dressed. Paul walked right up to her.

"Tom will accompany you to the cottage viewing this morning, as you can see, I can't drive today. Bring Thiago here on Saturday, Nikki will not be here. But don't you dare try pulling a stunt like you did this morning ever, ever again. I love Nikki and I do. Not. Want. You. Back. Got it?" he snapped.

Valentina looked contrite. She gave a brief nod before leaving the house. She was sitting in her car waiting when Tom appeared from the house. He pointed towards his silver Mercedes and Valentina got out and walked over to join him.

Nikki turned to face Paul. "You should have called me when you hurt yourself last night," she said.

"Honestly, there was no need. Tom was with me, and Chris needed you more. But the bare faced cheek of that woman!"

Nikki was still recovering from the shock herself. "She's got some front that's for sure. I didn't know what to think when I walked in and saw her wearing your shirt. She was obviously hoping that I'd storm out of the house before you came downstairs," she said amazed at Valentina's brazen plan.

A little while later the gate buzzed again. It was Derek this time who had offered to help Chris with the move. He was finding it a little difficult to adjust to being retired and jumped at the opportunity to get out of the house for a while. Nikki had been watching out for them, she was so excited about Chris's move to the folly. A couple of hours later the removal van turned up. Richard, Janet, Paul, and Nikki all mucked in to get everything put into place. They had seen Valentina returning with Tom and she had quickly driven away after throwing a quizzical look across to the activity going on at the bungalow. Paul and Nikki had told them all about what had happened this morning and everyone was totally disgusted at her actions. Tom joined them all once he had parked his car.

"How did the viewing go?" asked Paul.

"OK, I think. Valentina was a bit subdued to start with but soon cheered up when she realised what a lovely cottage you were going to buy for her. Oh, and towards the end she stroked my arm and suggested that we went out to dinner sometime soon," Tom replied.

"Oh, the cheek of the woman!" said Janet, flushing bright red feeling angry at the impact Valentina was having on her family once again.

"I think I love her," teased Tom.

"Don't you dare," warned Janet.

Soon, Chris was all settled in his new home, surrounded by his friends and family. Nikki was pleased to have him living close by. Life would be perfect if it weren't for a certain person.

CHAPTER THIRTEEN

A couple of days later, Richard, Tom, Paul and Nikki had been present when the Tudor building and the artist's cottages had passed all the health and safety inspections.

The ground floor of the Tudor building was made up of two modern-looking classrooms with whiteboards put up around the rooms and an overhead projector for use by the tutors. Although so far this building had been earmarked for just residential courses, Paul was keen to allow local schools and colleges to make use of them too. He was enthusiastic about the arts, and he wanted to inspire people to tap into their creative skills.

Upstairs, the rooms for the visitors were the same as the bedrooms in the art castle. Clean and light with navy-blue furnishings.

"I'm really impressed with the way everything is looking,"

said Richard. "Nikki, your team have done a cracking job for us."

Nikki beamed. She and Chris had always set extremely high standards, which was how they had managed to keep so many of their contracts. The guys on their team had known how important the Archer's Folly project was and now the results were there for everyone to see.

They travelled over to the cottages. Nikki absolutely adored the whimsical nature of this area of the folly. The pastel paintwork colour on the outside of each cottage matched the colour of the paintwork on the doors and paintwork inside. Light oak flooring was fitted throughout. There was a light grey leather two-seater sofa with a matching armchair in each lounge with a glass coffee table. All very sleek and modern. There were framed photographs of the separate phases of the building and decorating of the cottages on the walls. White fitted kitchens had been installed with light grey matching utensils, kettles, and toasters. Upstairs, smart white bathrooms had been fitted with a free-standing bath overlooking the wildflower garden nearby. King-size beds had been placed in the bedrooms with navy-blue curtains and duvet covers which contrasted beautifully with the pastel woodwork.

"I could quite happily live in one of these myself," said Nikki.

"Not happening. I need you to look after me." Paul dodged

out of the way when Nikki took a swipe at his arm.

"So next week it's the turn of the artisan square and the diner to be inspected and then we'll be pretty much ready to let everyone move in," said Tom. "All of the contracts have been signed now by the people moving into the square and they're all keen to get cracking as soon as possible."

"I'm looking forward to seeing the diner," said Nikki. "Matt and the guys have been working on it while I was busy helping Dad."

"You're going to love it," replied Paul. "Another one of my crazy ideas becoming a reality."

As they all made their way back towards the buggy's, Matt walked over towards them.

"Hi, Matt, how did it go this morning?" asked Nikki.

Matt and his new fiancée Erica had been to meet a financial advisor about getting a mortgage. The property owner was selling the flat they were currently renting, and it was exactly the push they had needed to try and buy a place of their own.

"Um, good thanks," replied Matt, not making eye contact with any of them. It was unlike him. He just stood there with his hands in his pockets and kicking at the ground.

"Is there a problem?" asked Paul.

Matt exhaled. "This morning after our meeting we went for lunch at the seafood restaurant and chose to sit outside. There was a couple with a little boy in a pushchair sitting at the table next to us. They attracted my attention because they were speaking Spanish."

"Matt's dad is Spanish so he can speak the lingo," explained Nikki.

Matt nodded. "Firstly, my ears pricked up when the man called the woman Valentina and the boy Thiago. Nikki had told me about the latest development in your lives. However, I was puzzled because the little boy kept calling the man Daddy."

"Interesting," said Paul staring intently at Matt as he told them his story.

"The man's name was Guillermo and Valentina referred to him as her husband a couple of times He was asking how much longer they would have to stay in this country, and she said that once the cottage had been purchased for her and some regular financial support had been arranged she would leave it a while and then make an excuse to sell up and return to Spain. Paul, I think you're being conned," said Matt with conviction.

"Paul, when you carried out the DNA test Valentina didn't seal the envelope did she? She just stuffed everything into her bag. I bet her husband provided another sample and that was the one she sent off to the testing company!" exclaimed Nikki.

Paul scowled and took his phone out of his pocket. "I'm going to ring her and send her packing once and for all," he said, angry that he had allowed himself to be taken in by Valentina's lies.

Tom put a hand on his arm to stop him. "No, let's get all our ducks in a row. When Valentina comes round on Saturday to start your bonding with Thiago, try and get a sample from him. Then send the test away to get the definitive result that he's not your son. After that we'll all join you in sending her away for the last time. I'll put a stop to the purchase of the cottage too."

Paul turned to face Matt. "You don't know how much this means to me. Thank you. I could have been tied to that woman for life if you hadn't overheard their conversation. Why don't you go and view the cottage in Honesty and if you like it I would like to gift it to you and Erica."

"What a lovely thing to do!" exclaimed Nikki as Matt stood there looking stunned.

"Let's face it, the cost of a cottage compared to the thousands of pounds Valentina would have fleeced off me for the next twenty years is nothing in the greater scheme of things. Consider it my wedding present to you both," said Paul.

"I...I don't know what to say," Matt stuttered. "Thank you very much. I can't believe this is happening to me," he said shaking his head in disbelief at this sudden turn of events.

"I'm going to phone Erica right now," he said still in a state of shock.

"Let's get back home," said Paul. "I've got a new DNA testing kit to order."

He turned to look at his dad who was still looking shocked at the news Matt had given them.

"Your poor mother, one minute she's getting her head around having a new grandson and now I'm going home to tell her that he isn't after all. She's been checking out Spanish conversation classes and buying some toys for the child to play with," said Richard.

"What a horrible mess." Tom shook his head.

Nikki's heart had lifted at the news that Thiago wasn't Paul's son. She wasn't sure she had the strength to have coped with it all. It would have put a massive strain on their relationship. She couldn't wait to see the back of Valentina.

When she and Paul got home he picked her up and swung her round the room in celebration at the news Matt had given them. "I can't believe it, this is fabulous news, but I'm going to find it very hard to act normally on Saturday," said Paul feeling overjoyed at the latest turn of events.

Nikki kissed him. "At least we know that it will be all over this time next week." She pulled a face. "But she originally suggested moving in here. That doesn't seem to fit in with the plan Matt heard. Plus, she made a pass at Tom when he took her to view the cottage."

"Oh, I know Valentina. If I had welcomed her back into

my life with open arms she would have left her husband like a shot. Before I found out about her other boyfriend I was financing a very lavish and comfortable lifestyle for her," said Paul struggling to believe that he had been cheated by her for a second time.

"What a horrible, horrible person." She opened her laptop. "I'm going to look online to see what I can find out about this Guillermo."

Paul rubbed his hands together. "What an excellent idea. I'm keen to know more about my love rival."

Nikki almost shoved him off the sofa. "Oh, very funny. But, where to start. I've never connected to any social media sites."

"Me neither but I'm sure we can give it a go. I remember Valentina used to talk about Instagram a lot so let's set up an account on that," said Paul.

Within a few minutes Nikki had joined up. "So, what is Valentina's full name?" she asked.

"It's Valentina Martinez," replied Paul.

Nikki typed it in and quickly found her. "Wow, she loves herself, doesn't she?" She scrolled through dozens of photos and selfies featuring Valentina.

"Just a bit, yes. Um, you might see quite a lot of photos with me in them," said Paul, knowing that this could be quite a painful experience for Nikki.

Nikki's heart thumped and her stomach contracted, she couldn't help feeling jealous when she did find photos of Paul and Valentina. In one they were sitting on the deck of a yacht just in front of a billowing sail. Paul was wearing an open white short-sleeved shirt and navy-blue tailored shorts and he had his arm around Valentina who was dressed in white shorts and a midriff-baring white tank top. They were both laughing and looking at each other with love in their eyes. Another photo showed Valentina standing on a white sandy beach with a cloudless azure sky above and the deep blue ocean behind. She was wearing the tiniest yellow bikini showing off her tanned Mediterranean skin. Paul was standing next to her in swim shorts in a matching yellow to the bikini, he was leaning on a surfboard smiling to the camera. Nikki's heart sank seeing the photos, she was very slim herself, but she wouldn't have the confidence to pose in a bikini like that.

"Do you miss that lifestyle?" she asked. Although it looked glamourous, she preferred the quiet life. Would Paul tire of that eventually and look for somebody more outgoing?

He shook his head. "No, I'm honestly very contented. There's nothing stopping us going on exotic holidays if we want to. Valentina constantly organised nights out and holidays. Don't get me wrong, we had a lot of fun, but it was so exhausting. I used to dream of the life I have now." Nikki knew in that moment that what he said was true. He kissed her. "I have never been happier."

Nikki relaxed then and soon found an album entitled "Mi Boda"

"Here we go, Valentina's wedding photos."

Valentina looked stunning in a fabulous, fitted wedding dress. Her husband Guillermo was a very handsome man sporting curly hair and a perfectly groomed beard.

"So, her husband is called Guillermo Morales. There's obviously some blurb about him but it's in Spanish of course."

"Let's copy and paste it into a translation tool," said Paul.

"Excellent idea," agreed Nikki.

Soon they were scanning through the translation.

"So, it seems that they've been friends since they were teenagers. He owns a tapas bar in Majorca. It doesn't look like he's super-rich or anything," said Nikki.

"No, that's probably why she's trying to con me," said Paul, who could feel his temper rising again.

"Look - photos of Thiago."

There, for all the world to see, were photos of the wedding couple sitting with a smiling child on their laps,

"Well, we have our proof now, but I agree with Tom. Let's get the DNA test done and then we'll definitely know that we can cut her loose. There's still an outside chance he is mine I suppose so at least we can put it all to bed then," said Paul, pleased that this would soon be all over.

When Valentina turned up with Thiago on Saturday morning she was full of smiles.

"Paul, the cottage is beautiful, we will be very happy living there," she said smugly.

Nikki had warned Paul to act normally but she could see the tension on his face as she sat at the breakfast bar on her laptop.

Valentina looked at Paul. "What is she doing here?" She glared at Nikki.

Nikki closed the laptop and stood up. "Don't worry, I'm leaving now," she said as she gave Paul a lingering kiss. She was spending the morning with Cleo and the children. Mike was off playing golf with Tom.

Cleo hugged her friend when she turned up. "How's it going over there?"

Nikki laughed. "She's very happy about the cottage but she just fell short of ordering me out of the house."

"Cheeky cow!"

"I don't care because it's nearly all over and then our life can go back to normal," said Nikki.

"So, what's the plan?" asked Cleo.

"Paul is planning to cut a couple of hairs from Thiago's head when Valentina leaves the room. He's absolutely seething but I made him promise to be civil and not make Valentina suspicious," replied Nikki.

Riley suddenly appeared and climbed up onto Nikki's lap.

"Hi, Riley, this is nice." Nikki blew a raspberry on the little boy's tummy making him chuckle. Ava came over holding the sketchbook Paul and Nikki had given her for her birthday.

"Look, Nikki, I've been drawing pictures of the garden," she said proudly.

Nikki balanced Riley carefully on her knee enjoying the cuddle and placed the sketchbook on the arm of the sofa next to her. Ava had drawn the swing set in the garden as well as a picture of her and Riley in the pink convertible.

"These are wonderful Ava," she said, and the little girl beamed with pride.

She tried to stop Nikki turning the page.

"Don't look at the next one, Riley scribbled with crayons," she sounded like she was about to cry.

"Now, Ava, we talked about this. Riley just wanted to draw because he was so impressed with your pictures," said Cleo.

"But it's my sketchbook," Ava argued.

"Yes, it is and now we've bought Riley his own drawing book, so he won't use your one now," replied Cleo firmly.

Riley wriggled off Nikki's lap and soon returned with a drawing book filled with squiggles drawn with crayons.

"Very good, Riley." Nikki smiled.

"But I'm the best," said Ava before flouncing off.

A little while later a text came from Paul.

Mission Accomplished.

Nikki showed Cleo. "I bet Paul will try and cut Valentina's visit short now he's got what he wanted," she said.

"How long was she expecting to stay?" asked Cleo.

"For as long as possible I'm guessing. She has Paul all to herself after all," replied Nikki.

After three hours, Paul decided to plead a migraine. "I'm sorry, Valentina, I really feel unwell. Come back again next week and in the meantime if I hear any news about the cottage I'll let you know," he said, hoping that she wouldn't see through his lie.

Valentina had pouted but nodded in agreement. She remembered that Paul had suffered from migraines from time to time. She tidied up the toys that Janet had bought earlier in the week. Thiago had enjoyed playing with them.

"You can take them with you if you like," said Paul.

"No, it will be nice for your son to have toys to play with here," replied Valentina.

Paul wondered round to meet up with Nikki, Cleo, and the children soon after Valentina and Thiago had left.

"Uncle Paul!" shouted Ava and Riley in glee as they jumped all over him.

He chased them around the garden for a little while before collapsing into a chair out of breath.

"Was it easy to snip some hair?" asked Cleo.

"It was really tense. Valentina popped to the loo, and I made my move. Thiago was playing with a car on the floor, and I leaned over with the scissors just as he turned to face me. I made a quick snip and he started to cry. I picked him up and just told Valentina that he was wondering where she had gone," Paul replied.

"I'll post the testing kit for you later on when I go shopping," offered Nikki.

"I couldn't wait, I got a courier to come and collect it. I paid for the fast-track service. It's nearly all over now," said Paul looking more relaxed than he had for a long time. He couldn't wait to confront Valentina with the truth.

CHAPTER FOURTEEN

It was the final day of the Health and Safety inspections at the folly. Richard, Paul, Mike, Tom, Matt, and Nikki all stood in the artisan square.

Richard looked at his notebook. "We have a few actions. They want an additional fire door installed in both the glass art and ceramic units, I've already made the relevant phone calls and they'll be fitted tomorrow morning. We'll have to make sure that regular fire drills take place and arrange Fire Marshall training for the unit owners. Somebody from the local fire brigade will come down to organise it. But apart from that we're good to go," he said smiling broadly at everyone.

"So, who is moving into each unit?" asked Matt

Mike looked at his notes. "Units one and two are being used by the Womack Brothers Art Studios, one for glass blowing and the other for stained-glass art."

"That sounds really interesting," said Nikki making a mental note to spend some time watching them. She had never seen glass blowing being carried out before.

"The third large one on this side is going to be used by someone making wood carvings, furniture and decorative gifts. Then the four smaller units across the top here are a silver jewellery maker, a costume designer, a floral artist and a card and calligraphy company. Finally, the last three larger units down the other side will house an upcycling company and ceramic artists. The potentially biggest draw for us Mitch and Mabel will be taking over the third and final unit," said Mike, looking round at the group.

"They make wonderful, scented candles, wax melts and soaps," said Nikki who loved scented things as Paul had discovered with the arrival of her enormous collection of candles and reed diffusers now in situ around the house.

Mitch and Mabel were an up-and-coming company quickly making a name for themselves in the world of fragrances for homes and businesses.

Mike smiled. "Cleo is thrilled about them coming too." "Our landscape gardener actually knows a lot about beekeeping, and he is going to set up the hives behind the square. It was Nikki's idea, and we're hoping to produce Archer's Folly Honey."

"Well, I thought it would make sense to utilise the

wildflower garden," Nikki added.

"Good call, Nikki," said Richard.

"Let's look at the apartments now," said Tom. "I haven't been in any of them since before the storm."

They trouped up the stairs to one of the apartments in one of the larger units, these would have three bedrooms while the others just had one. The walls had all been painted in a rich creamy colour. There were rustic oak floors with matching ceiling fans. Indigo blue painted Shaker kitchens had been fitted. There was a lovely space for comfortable sofas and chairs in front of a wood-burning stove set in a red stone fireplace. The bedrooms were large with the same cream walls but with a luxurious deep pile cream carpet to match. The bathrooms in keeping with the others around the entire site were white with a free-standing bath as well as a separate shower.

"Well, once again I take my hat off to you and your team," said Richard in admiration. "Matt be well assured that we will definitely use you again in the future. You obviously have the same vision and work ethic as Nikki and Chris."

Matt nodded and smiled over at Nikki. "I learned from the best and I fully intend to keep the standards high and keep improving."

Chris had always taken the time to personally train up any new starters in his decorating company. He didn't believe in short cuts and always used high quality materials.

Paul rubbed his hands together — something that Nikki had come to recognise as his way of displaying excitement. "I think it's time to unveil the diner," he said gleefully.

Nikki had not been allowed anywhere near the diner, so Paul's excitement was catching.

They all walked through the double gates out of the square and across to where a giant cover had been erected to obscure the diner from sight. Only Paul, Mike and Richard had seen the finished article and they grinned when they saw the anticipation on Tom and Nikki's faces. Paul walked to the side and pulled the curtain away from the front of the diner.

"Ta-Da!" he sang.

Nikki and Tom looked impressed. It was a bright red building with a large window on either side of the door. There was a huge sign on the roof which said, "Archer's Diner." In front of the diner was a bright red car.

"This is a 1957 vintage Chevy Corvette," announced Paul. "Isn't she a beauty?"

"Wow!" said Nikki, finally finding her voice. "This definitely looks like a nineteen fifties diner."

Inside everything was either chrome or bright red with several booths set around the diner. There were high stools set against the counter with milk shake machines, fizzy drink taps and an ice cream dispenser. There was an old-fashioned jukebox, too.

Paul popped a pound coin in the slot. "This works like a dream!" he said as Elvis Presley's Jail House Rock filled the diner.

"I love it!" said Nikki. "I'm glad you made me wait for the big reveal."

Matt had worked on it with just two other guys from the team who had all been sworn to secrecy about their final piece of work at the folly. However, he had only decorated the building when it was empty, and he too was impressed by the way it had been kitted out.

"Who's going to run the diner?" asked Richard.

"Well, down in Honesty there's a lovely restaurant by the pond called Heart of the Home. Cleo was speaking to Zoe, the daughter of the owners who has worked there for several years, and she mentioned that she wanted to broaden her horizons. Armed with that knowledge we offered her the chance to manage the diner and live in the flat above," said Paul. "She was ecstatic and agreed immediately."

"We should hold a welcome to Archer's Folly event for the new arrivals," said Nikki.

Paul swung round to face her with a smile. "What a brilliant idea. Do you think that given that there isn't an awful lot of time maybe you and Cleo could organise something?"

"I really think that we could. I'll speak to Cleo as soon as we go back up to the house," said Nikki with ideas already starting to buzz in her head.

Over the next two days Cleo and Nikki spent hours planning for the opening of the folly. Every time Mike or Paul got anywhere close to them they closed their notebooks and whispered furtively to each other.

"How's the party planning coming on?" asked Paul stretching to try and look over Nikki's shoulder.

"Once again, go away!" instructed Cleo "You're both as bad as the children."

"Let's just say you'll be very pleased with the results," said Nikki.

There was a buzz at the gate and Paul could see that it was a motorcycle courier. He suddenly felt very cold and clammy. This was the news they had all been waiting for. He opened the door, took the package, and went back to where Nikki, Mike and Cleo were sitting.

"Do you want me to open it again?" asked Nikki.

Paul shook his head. "I'm feeling a lot more hopeful about this result." He tore the top of the envelope off and pulled out the sheet of paper. He closed his eyes briefly. "Thiago is not my son. Oh, thank goodness, now we can get rid of Valentina for good," he said feeling relieved that it was almost over. His eyes filled with tears of relief and as walked over to Nikki he could see that she was also crying but smiling at the same time.

"When are you going to ask her to come over?" asked Cleo.

"There's no time like the present," replied Paul, taking out his phone and selecting Valentina's number. She didn't take too long to answer. "Hi, Valentina, would you be able to come over to see me today? You could? Great, see you soon."

Valentina had heard the happiness in Paul's voice and had presumed that things might be swinging in her favour after all and just under an hour later she had arrived at the house without Thiago in tow. She was obviously hoping for time alone with Paul and had dressed herself in a low-cut navy-blue dress which clung to all her curves. She was clearly taken aback by the sight of the others sitting around the room.

"You wanted to see me?" she asked looking round at everyone.

"Most definitely," said Paul. "The other day a friend of ours was eating lunch at the seafood restaurant in the town. They were sitting outside." Apart from a slight tic in one of Valentina's eyes, she remained expressionless. "Our friend speaks Spanish fluently and he mentioned that a Spanish speaking couple with a young child were sitting at the next table to them. We thought it was more than a coincidence that the woman was called Valentina with a child called Thiago. When were you planning to tell me that you were married, Valentina?"

Mike suppressed a smile, he thought Paul sounded like

someone off a legal drama on the television.

"No! Your friend was wrong. It wasn't me; I'm not married. It must have been a coincidence," Valentina fired back. "And Thiago is your son, you have the DNA evidence," she countered.

"Hmm, well, then we remembered that you didn't actually seal the envelope here after I gave you my swab test. We think that you switched my swab with your husband's to try and convince me that Thiago was my son," said Paul, enjoying himself now.

"Again, not true," said Valentina frowning at the unfolding situation.

Nikki couldn't believe how brazenly Valentina was lying. "We found your wedding photos on Instagram," she shouted. "How long can you keep this pretence up?"

Valentina looked at Nikki with real hatred in her eyes. "Paul won't keep you for long. You're not his type at all, you have no class," she sneered before turning back to Paul. "OK, so I admit to being married but Thiago really is your son."

Paul shook his head. "No, he's not Valentina. When you came round last Saturday, I cut a lock of Thiago's hair to send away for another DNA test."

"How dare you do that to my son!" she spat back.

"Well, I did and here are the results that arrived earlier today," Paul replied. He showed her the letter confirming the negative DNA result and she tore it up into little pieces and threw them onto the floor. "Now, I want you to get out and never come anywhere near me or my family ever again, do you understand? I could have phoned the police about your attempt to extort money from me. But I don't want to prolong this any further. I feel deeply sorry for Guillermo. Now get out!" Paul shouted.

Nikki, Cleo, and Mike waved as Paul guided Valentina back towards the front door and stood and watched her drive away out of his life, this time hopefully for ever. As he closed the door behind her, he put his back to the door and slid down to the floor sobbing uncontrollably. Nikki heard him and dashed out. She sat down beside him and put her arm around him until he stopped crying. He wiped the tears from his face.

"I'm sorry," he mumbled into Nikki's shoulder. "It's all been a bit intense." He wiped the tears that were falling from her eyes too.

"It's been very intense," she agreed with a deep sigh.

Paul stood up and pulled Nikki up to join him. They walked out to the kitchen. Mike and Cleo had tactfully left through the kitchen door leaving Paul and Nikki alone. A little while later the whole family returned ready to celebrate the good news. Janet was blinking rapidly to try and prevent herself from crying, but the tears escaped anyway.

"I'm sorry. I've been keeping myself awake at night

worrying about being a good grandmother to a child who didn't know me and who didn't even speak English."

Paul hugged his mother tightly. He was furious that Valentina had managed to confuse and upset his mum like this. But at least it was all over.

"Can we make pizzas?" asked Ava sensing the celebratory air as Tom popped the cork from a nicely chilled bottle of champagne.

"Yes!" replied Paul and Nikki together smiling at each other with relief at the prospect of life returning to normal once again.

"With pineapple?" continued Ava.

"Definitely with pineapple." Nikki laughed while Paul just pulled a face.

She kept hugging Paul glad that Valentina was finally gone for good. Now they could concentrate on the opening of the folly.

CHAPTER FIFTEEN

A week after Valentina's plan had been rumbled, the new residents of the artisan square moved in. While Paul had concentrated on creating the quirky mix of buildings at the folly, Mike had ensured that the right infrastructure was in place to accommodate the vans and cars belonging to the people taking over the units. To this end he had built a tarmac road that ran around the outside of the square and a car park for the new tenants strategically hidden behind a colourful shrubbery. As they had made it a rule that no vehicles could travel any further into the folly grounds, some new buggies were parked up for use by the tenants to drive around on the orange brick road.

Nikki and Cleo had set up a gazebo in the centre of the square with ice boxes filled with wine, beer and juice ready to greet the new arrivals. They had put bunting around the gazebo to try and make it look nice and welcoming. Paul was very excited. This was the beginning of the fulfilment of his dream, Archer's Folly.

The first removal van parked up outside the units being taken over by the Womack brothers. A couple who appeared to be in their early forties jumped out of the car which had parked in front of the van. The man was very tall and slightly built with long blonde hair which had been tied in a ponytail. His wife was also very tall and slim but with short dark hair.

Paul, Cleo, and Nikki walked forward to greet them.

"Hi, welcome to Archer's Folly, I'm Paul Archer. You've been dealing with my brother Tom up until now so it's nice to meet you properly."

Tom had been responsible for the signing of all the contracts for everybody wanting to move into the artisan square.

"Hi, Paul," said the man, smiling. "I'm Ollie Womack, this is my wife Vanessa, and sitting in the car sulking is our daughter Sophie."

"What's upset Sophie?" asked Nikki

"We've ruined her life apparently by moving away from the town where all her friends are," said Vanessa, sounding stressed.

"Setting up here at Archer's Folly was something we just had to do," said Ollie. "It looks like such a wonderful place to work and live in. Sophie's having driving lessons now so if she passes her test we'll buy her a car and then she can visit her friends. Although I could easily imagine them wanting to come here for a visit."

"Are you the glassblower?" asked Mike.

"No, I'm the stained-glass man," replied Ollie. "Arlo is moving in tomorrow."

The removal men started to unload the lorry and carry boxes up the stairs.

"Would you like a drink before you start moving in?" asked Nikki.

"I wouldn't say no to a cold beer," he replied.

"A beer would work for me too," replied Vanessa, finally allowing herself to smile.

They stood enjoying their drinks and the conversation flowed easily as Paul outlined his dreams for the folly. Then, they decided to crack on with moving into their new home.

"We'll leave you to it," said Paul. "If you need anything you can find our contact numbers on the wall by the storage room."

Vanessa and Ollie watched as Paul, Nikki, Mike and Cleo walked away.

"They all seem really nice," said Vanessa feeling relaxed for the first time that day.

Ollie nodded in agreement. "They do," he replied, putting

an arm round his wife. "And don't worry, Sophie will soon come round."

They busied themselves arranging their furniture and finding a home for everything. Vanessa was thrilled to see a small hamper that had been left in the kitchen which held a loaf of bread and a fruit cake that Cleo had bought from the bakery in Honesty. There was a bottle of red wine, jam, coffee, an assortment of tea bags and a box of chocolates. In the fridge Vanessa found a bottle of champagne, milk, juice, eggs, ham, and cheese. In the bathroom was another gift basket holding luxury bath oil, soaps, and shampoo.

"How thoughtful," Vanessa mused as Sophie finally appeared.

"Where's my room?" she asked while clicking furiously away on her phone.

"Sophie, can you put your phone down for even a short while? We could really do with some help putting everything away," said Vanessa, feeling frustrated.

"Stop nagging, Mum," Sophie replied.

Vanessa pointed to the door on the other side of the bathroom.

"That's your room. Your boxes are in there. Now go and unpack them please."

Sophie huffed and wandered off towards her room.

Vanessa went in search of her husband and found him next

door supervising the removal men as they carried up all of Arlo's furniture and belongings. His brother was driving down in the morning in a van holding all their glasswork tools and equipment.

Another removal van arrived at the opposite side of the square, and this was followed by an old bright yellow Volkswagen Beetle covered in stickers of brightly coloured butterflies.

Two women jumped out. The shorter one of the two had bright red hair and was dressed in a pair of olive-coloured dungarees with a short-sleeved white T-shirt underneath. She wore an olive-green headscarf to complete the nineteen forties land girl image. Her red, glittering lipstick was the same colour as her hair. The other woman had platinum blonde hair which was tied in a high ponytail with a red scarf. She had brightly coloured tattoo sleeves on both of her arms. She wore a pair of dark denim cropped jeans with a red and black halter neck top. They both smiled as Cleo, Nikki and Paul approached them.

"Hi," the woman with the red hair greeted them. "My name's Red and this is my wife Pippa."

As they shook hands Nikki spoke up. "So, Red, I detect an American accent, whereabouts do you hail from?"

"New York, born and bred," Red replied. "I was called Red from an early age by my Grandpa because my hair was a carroty colour, nowhere near as bright as this and the name just stuck all the way through school and college. My real name's Kendra."

"Welcome to Archer's Folly. It's nice to meet you both," said Paul as Cleo handed them a nicely chilled glass of white wine each.

"So, you're taking over one small and one large unit," confirmed Mike who had joined the greeting party.

"That's right," said Pippa. "I make vintage style clothing and I only needed a small unit for that. Red here needs all the space she can get to carry out all of her furniture upcycling."

"I create lots of dust when I plane and rub down the furniture and then I wanted a section to varnish and a section to paint," said Red.

"Hence your request for extra ventilation to be installed," said Mike.

"Absolutely," agreed Red.

Red and Pippa were going to live in the apartment above the larger unit while Damien the beekeeper was going to live in the apartment above the smaller unit. He was also the folly's landscape gardener and managed the wildflower garden, shrubberies, topiaries, and orchards.

"It's so nice to meet you both," said Nikki. "We're holding a welcome party on Saturday so everybody can really get to know each other then."

"Sounds like fun," said Pippa.

"Is anybody else moving in today?" Paul asked as they left Red and Pippa to settle in.

"Yes, Heather the silver jewellery maker is due to arrive today. She's travelling down from her home in Scotland," replied Mike.

Just as he spoke, a self-drive rental van arrived, and an older man jumped out of the driving seat while a younger woman who looked to be in her mid-twenties got out too.

"Hello, I'm Gregory McBain and this is my daughter Heather," the man said in a broad Scottish accent.

"Hi," they all replied.

Heather was incredibly thin with porcelain white skin and long black hair. She was pretty but her body language was very closed. Her eyes darted around nervously, and she didn't smile.

"Hello," she said in a small voice.

Nikki's heart went out to her, she was clearly very shy.

"Welcome to the Folly." She held her hand out which Heather shook limply.

"How long are you staying for?" Paul asked Gregory.

"I'm going to hang around for a couple of days and help Heather to get set up. I've got the van until Friday, then I'll make the trek back home again. It's a ten-hour drive up to Aberdeen. We stopped off at my sister's house in the Midlands last night just to break up the journey," he said.

"Well, it's great to meet you both." Paul smiled. "We hope

you're very happy here at Archer's Folly, Heather."

Heather gave a small smile which disappeared quickly.

"She's a bit strange," said Mike once they were out of earshot.

"I think she's just very shy," replied Nikki. "Once she's settled in I'm sure she'll come out of her shell."

They walked over to the diner which had opened at the start of the week and had been a big hit with the staff at the hotel and conference centre. It was only going to open for breakfast and lunch as they hadn't really seen a need for night-time opening.

Zoe smiled warmly at them as they trooped inside. She was in her thirties and was loving having somewhere of her own to manage as she had only ever worked for her parents in Honesty. Damien was sitting on one of the high stools at the counter drinking a milkshake.

"Hi, guys, how are all you today?" she asked

"All good," replied Nikki as she eyed up Damien's drink. "Could I have a chocolate milkshake please?"

Mike and Paul weren't very keen on milkshakes, so they ordered a couple of cokes.

"Damien, have the bees arrived yet?" asked Paul "I love the area you've created for the hives."

Damien had put up white fencing with a gate to surround the beehive houses he had installed. There was also a shed that he had painted white which held his beekeeper protective clothing and smoking equipment.

"Thanks, Paul, the bees are arriving at the beginning of next week. I'll just have to maintain the hives over the winter months, let the bees get used to their new location. Next summer we will have our first batches of Archer's Folly Honey," said Damien.

"Sounds great," replied Paul.

"I've got loads of work to do in the meantime, maintaining the shrubberies and looking after the topiary in the main driveway," continued Damien.

"Here are your drinks everyone," said Zoe, placing them on the counter.

She made eye contact with Damien who smiled at her making her blush. Nikki thought that Archer's Folly might have worked its magic again, and that romance was in the air.

The next day Nikki and Cleo waited to greet the remaining new arrivals. Paul would join them shortly. He was meeting one of the new tenants over at the conference centre. Constance Browning was a friend of his who specialised in extremely high-end flower displays. She had been the first person to sign up for a unit in the artisan square as she didn't enjoy being based in London anymore.

The door to the wood carving unit was already open and a man who appeared to be in his fifties was busy putting his equipment into place.

"Good morning," said Cleo. "Welcome to Archer's Folly."

The man stopped what he was doing and walked across to greet them. He was very distinguished looking with a full head of silver hair and when he smiled the laughter lines around his blue eyes crinkled. He was wearing a pair of light blue jeans and a plaid shirt with the sleeves rolled up.

"Good morning to you too," he replied, leaning forward to shake everybody's hands.

"James Pullen at your service, I arrived about seven o'clock this morning, couldn't wait to move in and get set up," he said.

"Do you need help with anything?" asked Mike.

James nodded towards Ollie who was standing in the doorway. "Ollie here has been very neighbourly and helped me to move my lathe into position," he said.

"My pleasure James, just give me a shout if you need anything else," said Ollie before he disappeared back outside.

"Thank you for the lovely hamper it was most welcome," said James.

"It's our pleasure," replied Cleo. "We want everyone to feel at home here."

James's attention moved outside.

"Some more new arrivals. It's so nice that we are all starting out together here."

Nikki nodded. "I think so too, it's like the first day of a new school term."

"It's Mitch and Mabel," said Cleo.

"Well, James, it was lovely to meet you. Just call us if you need anything and we look forward to getting to know more about you at the party we are throwing for you all on Saturday."

"Thank you," said James. "I'm looking forward to it."

They walked over to greet Mitch and Mabel who were chatting to Red and Pippa.

"Morning, everyone." said Nikki smiling.

"Good morning," the others replied together.

"I'm absolutely thrilled to have Mitch and Mabel moving in here too," raved Red.

"Our apartment is full of their products, and now we don't even have to order online. And we all have a quirky taste in clothing too."

Pippa nodded in agreement.

Mitch chuckled. He was a very tall, well-built man with short brown hair. He sported a magnificent well waxed handlebar moustache. He was wearing a red and white striped blazer with a red patterned shirt beneath. He had on a pair of tight white jeans with highly polished cherry red winklepickers on his feet.

"It's lovely to meet everybody," he said with a broad smile on his face. "I can tell we're going to have a lot of fun living and working here."

Nikki looked at Mabel. "I love what you're wearing," she said in admiration.

Mabel was wearing a psychedelic multi-patterned mini dress with a string of flowers in her long auburn hair. She wore a pair of white boots and a pair of pink heart-shaped sunglasses to finish the nineteen sixties look.

"Thank you." Mabel smiled back. "I love to play around with distinctive styles, it's a lot of fun. This looks like it is going to be a fantastic place to work in, much more creative than the industrial estate we had been working out of," she said.

"Surely you can't make everything you sell here?" asked Cleo. "You're so well-known now; you would have to be working twenty-four-hour days."

"You're quite right, we couldn't manage all on our own," said Mitch. "This is going to be our new workshop where we can experiment and develop new products. Our manufacturing will continue in the place we have just moved out of."

"Ah, I see," said Cleo. "Well, we're all glad you have chosen to get nice and creative here at the folly."

Just then Paul walked over with a smartly dressed woman, her blond hair elegantly styled in a chignon. Nikki smiled, she really liked Constance. Paul had known her for years and they had all met up for drinks and a bite to eat occasionally.

"Hi, Constance," she said.

Constance smiled as she walked over. "Hello there," she said in a very posh accent. "Mitchell, long time no see."

Mitch stared at her for a moment while he tried to work out where he knew her from. Then the penny dropped.

"Connie! How marvellous to see you again after all this time," he said.

Cleo noticed a dark look quickly cross Mabel's face before her smile returned, was it irritation or jealousy? She wasn't too sure.

"How do you two guys know each other?" asked Paul.

"My father's a racehorse trainer, and he trains Connie's father's horses," Mitch explained. "Very successfully, I hasten to add."

Constance nodded in agreement. "Daddy loves horse racing and is proud to have owned two winners at Ascot and three at the Grand National over the years. It's so nice to see you again Mitchell and congratulations to the two of you for your successful brand."

"Thank you." Mabel smiled, clearly more relaxed in Connie's company now.

"Are your children here today?" asked Cleo.

"No, they're with my sister until tomorrow," explained Mabel. "We just want to get moved in and sorted out first. They're going to love all the green open spaces around here, much better than living in a town."

"Who's moving into the remaining units?" asked Red.

"Well, the large one is being taken over by a couple who make ceramics, they are due to arrive tomorrow. The small unit is for a couple who make cards and provide a calligraphy service. They're due to arrive later today," replied Paul. "We have a great mix of arts and crafts; I'm excited about it."

"We're looking forward to the party," said Pippa.

"Cleo and Nikki have been busy with the party planning, and I think we'll be in for a fun time on Saturday," replied Paul unable to keep the huge grin from his face. Everything he had planned for was finally happening

CHAPTER SIXTEEN

Cleo and Nikki were up early on Saturday morning knowing that they were in for a busy day. The party was due to begin at two o'clock and the invitation had been extended to the staff who worked at the conference centre and hotel as well as the contractors who had worked so hard to get the folly ready.

Janet and Richard had invited everyone over for an early family breakfast and soon they were all gathered enjoying the croissants, fruit, and pastries. Ava and Riley were already excited about the party and Cleo knew that their grandparents were going to be quite frazzled looking after them until it started.

Mike and Paul walked down to the folly with Nikki and Cleo ready to help with organising everything.

"We have some trucks arriving in the next half hour," said

Cleo. "They're bringing fairground rides for both adults and children. We want them to be placed in the area in front of the diner alongside the square. Could you supervise that for us please?"

"Of course, no problem but let's go and introduce ourselves to the late arrivals to the square in the meantime," suggested Paul.

They walked into the square, it was already a hive of activity with the inhabitants chatting and laughing enjoying morning coffee together. Paul was thrilled, this was exactly the sort of atmosphere he had imagined. There were also some unfamiliar faces amongst them.

"Hi, guys, I'm Paul Archer," he said, shaking hands with the couple who had been chatting to James. The man was very distinguished looking with flecks of grey at the edge of his black hair. He wore a shirt brightly patterned with coloured birds. His wife was very tall and slim with curly brown hair, she was wearing a white sundress and a huge white floppy hat to protect her from the sun.

"Hello," said the man. "I'm Jabulani Afumba and this is my wife Fearne."

Fearne smiled. "This place is fabulous; everyone is so friendly and welcoming."

"What style of ceramics do you like to produce?" asked Nikki. She had always been interested in ceramic design.

"Twenty years ago, I went out to South Africa with my sister for a holiday. I met Jabulani in the shop where he was selling the items that he made. We fell in love, got married and there I stayed until earlier this year when we returned to the UK. Our ceramics are an eclectic mix of African and British designs," Fearne replied looking at her husband with love in her eyes, They were clearly a very happy couple.

"I'm looking forward to seeing your work," replied Nikki. "I bet you'll get some inspiration from everything here at the folly too."

"I'm sure we will," said Jabulani with a friendly smile.

Another couple wandered over, eager to introduce themselves too.

"Good morning, I'm William and this is Maxine my wife," the man said. They were in their early fifties. William was heavily built and appeared to be slightly out of breath when he spoke. He was wearing a pair of jeans and a way too small T-shirt which rode up over his large stomach. In contrast Maxine was slim with very curly blond hair and wearing a pair of denim shorts and a yellow floaty short-sleeved blouse. They were both smiling broadly obviously pleased to be moving into their new home.

"Good morning, and welcome to Archer's Folly," said Paul. "I hope you're settling in well and looking forward to the party this afternoon."

He frowned when he saw Nikki winking at William and Maxine.

"Paul, the trucks have arrived," called Mike from the entrance to the square.

"OK, on my way," Paul replied, still wondering what association Nikki had with the new arrivals. He was sure that they hadn't known each other previously. Time would tell he supposed.

Everyone worked hard over the next few hours. The fairground rides were in position. For the children there was an animal roundabout, a mini-Ferris wheel, and a spinning cups ride. There was also a trailer with a soft play area inside. For everybody else there was a waltzer, dodgems and a chair o plane. Added attractions included a coconut shy, a duck hooking game and a high striker strongman challenge. There was also a Velcro football net, a crazy golf course and a giant inflatable slide.

Zoe had been busy in the diner all morning making sandwiches, and drinks for the people working hard to get everything set up in time. The diner would remain open for the duration of the party. Cleo had hired two street food vendors which would be supplying Mexican and Caribbean food. There was also a stall supplying popcorn, candyfloss, and mini doughnuts.

Nikki was supervising the construction of a stage over by

the lake and there was a crew of people setting up microphones, speakers, and lights.

Mike and Paul were intrigued by what entertainment would be appearing on the stage as some serious kit was being set up there.

Sophie was in one of her bad moods again. Ollie and Vanessa had told her that she wasn't allowed to go into town to meet her friends. They felt that she should go to the party along with everybody else but had said that she could invite two of her friends to go too. She stormed off to her bedroom to call them.

"It's so unfair!" she told Izzie and Chelsea. "As soon as I'm eighteen they won't be able to stop me doing exactly what I want. At least you're coming to the stupid party too, I bet it's really lame."

However, when Sophie ventured outside she felt excited at the sight of the rides and got caught up in the atmosphere and instantly sent photos to her friends who responded with happy emojis.

"Nikki, you look beautiful," said Paul as she came downstairs after getting changed for the party. Nikki was wearing a green gingham sundress which matched the colour of her eyes with her hair styled with a single plait.

"You scrub up pretty nicely yourself, and we're colour coordinated too," Nikki replied, looking at Paul's shirt and thinking for the millionth time how gorgeous he was.

The doorbell rang and they opened it to an impatient Ava. "Hurry up! We don't want to miss the party," she said excitedly.

"Party!" shouted Riley who was sitting in his pushchair. It would have taken forever to walk with him down to the folly.

"Let's go then," said Paul with a smile. "The official launch of Archer's Folly."

Tom walked down with them while Richard, Janet and Chris drove down in a buggy.

It was already quite crowded when they arrived, and the DJ Nikki and Cleo had hired was getting the party started from his podium which had been set up at the side of the diner. Paul jumped up onto the podium and took the microphone.

"Hello, everybody, and welcome to the Archer's Folly launch party! I want to say a big thank you to everybody who has worked so hard to make my dream a reality. Big thanks to my lovely family who have put up with my foul moods at times. But I want to give a special thank you to my lovely partner Nikki for all her support, I love you so much. And of course, big thanks to Cleo who has also been amazing," he said feeling quite emotional.

Nikki flushed when everybody turned to look in her

direction and she gave a little regal wave which a laughing Cleo and Mike quickly copied.

"Anyway, I want you all to enjoy today and I declare the party officially OPEN!" said Paul with a big grin on his face.

Everybody cheered and soon there were queue's forming at the rides.

Mitch and Mabel walked over to Cleo and Mike with their two children in tow.

"Hi," said Mabel. "We would like you to meet Noah who is eight and Daisy who is five."

"I'm five, too." Ava jumped up and down.

"This is Ava and Riley, who is almost two," replied Cleo.

"Can we go to the fair now?" asked Noah, looking longingly over at the rides.

"Of course, we can, let's go," replied Mitch.

Ava and Daisy held hands as they skipped along together.

"Friends for life there I'm guessing," said Mabel. "Will Ava also be going to the school in Honesty?"

"Yup, half days next week, it will be nice for us to go together, it won't be so scary for them then," replied Cleo.

Paul and Nikki wandered round hand in hand thrilled that the party was running like clockwork.

"I haven't seen Heather yet today, have you?" asked Nikki.

"No, I don't think I have, and I spent a bit of time in the

square after the funfair was set up," replied Paul.

"I'm just going to pop to the square to check in on her," said Nikki. "She's so shy. I would hate for her to miss today's fun and games."

"OK, I'll see you later then." Paul kissed her, thinking how kind Nikki was.

Nikki walked back to the square and saw Heather through the window of her workshop with her head down clearly working on something. She tapped on the window and saw Heather jump up with a start.

"Hi, Heather, it's only me, Nikki."

"Hello, Nikki," Heather replied shyly.

"Don't you fancy coming to the party? We've laid on plenty of entertainment and it would be so nice if you could come along. It's a good chance to get to know everybody," said Nikki.

A nervous look crossed Heather's face. "I'm not much of a party person to be honest." Her eyes darted about anxiously.

Nikki didn't want to give up on her. "Tell you what. I'd like it if you could come along and keep me company for a while. Paul is busy mingling, and it would just be nice to wander around and people watch. Would you come with me?" she coaxed.

Heather hesitated then looked down at her jumper and jeans. "I'm not really dressed for a party; you look lovely by the way." Heather gave a brief smile.

"Thank you. I can wait for you if you want to go and get changed."

Heather considered her suggestion then gave a small nod. "OK, I'll come along. Give me a few minutes to get changed."

"Fantastic. I'll wait for you out here," Nikki replied.

A couple of minutes later Heather came down the stairs in a pair of white jeans and a pretty, long-sleeved blouse.

"You look great," said Nikki admiringly. "Come on let's go and enjoy the party."

She linked her arm through Heather's, and they set off towards the gate of the square.

They headed towards the pop-up cocktail bar where they both ordered a Tequila Sunrise marvelling as the two guys behind the bar threw bottles through the air before presenting them with their drinks. Just as they walked away Tom approached them.

"Hi, Tom," said Nikki. "Let me introduce you to Heather McBain, she makes silver jewellery. Heather this is Paul's brother Tom."

"Hi, Heather, lovely to meet you," said Tom.

Heather smiled briefly. "Hello, Tom." She was attracted to Tom's cheeky grin, the lovely dimples in his cheeks and his deep blue eyes.

Forget it Heather she thought. *You're sworn off men for life, remember?*

Tom comically waggled his eyebrows. "I'll join you on your walk around if that's OK, everyone seems to have disappeared, must be my new aftershave."

To their surprise, Heather burst out laughing. "You're funny," she said.

"Thanks, Heather…I think," replied Tom. He was attracted to her. She was a very pretty woman, but she was obviously unaware of this. When she smiled her eyes lit up. Heather was also painfully shy and that was something he wasn't used to. Women often threw themselves at him he was embarrassed to admit.

The sound of steel drums started up and people started to wander in the direction of the music so that they could go and watch. There was a group of ten young people and a slightly older man in the centre playing in perfect harmony. Cleo spotted Nikki, Heather and Tom and waved them over.

"This sounds fantastic," said Nikki, moving in rhythm to the music.

"The guy in the middle is my brother Gideon," said Cleo. "I can't wait to introduce him to you when they've finished playing."

She looked at Heather wanting to explain a little bit further about Gideon's work.

"He works at a club for youngsters in London, trying to

keep them out of gangs and off the streets. His idea to start a steel band was well received and now they get lots of requests to play at various events," she said.

"That's brilliant, Cleo, I love the idea of the club. We could do with more initiatives like that up in Scotland," said Heather swaying to the music.

Nikki couldn't wait to meet Gideon properly; she had heard so much about him from Cleo.

Paul wandered over at that moment and put his arm around Nikki's shoulder "Where's Mike?" she asked.

Paul laughed. "Ava keeps making him go on the inflatable slide with her. The stairs up are killing him."

Everyone else joined in with the laughter.

Cleo rocked Riley who was fast asleep in his pushchair, tired out from running around when the party started.

"Poor Mike, I should probably go and give him a break," she said just as he walked over giving a piggyback to a giggling Ava.

Just as it started to get dark the lights on the stage next to the lake switched on. Sophie and her friends looked over wondering what was happening.

Chelsea gave a loud screech. "Oh. My. God. Look!"

The other two girls turned to look where Chelsea was pointing, and they both gave a small scream.

"No freaking way!" Sophie held holding her phone up ready to film.

Setting up on the stage was the most popular boyband in the UK. Runners and Riders. Craig was the lead singer and Sophie and her friends loved him. They went dashing over to the stage.

"Craig, can we have some selfies with you?" She blushed. She couldn't believe she was speaking to her idol.

Craig, Dean and Marco jumped down from the stage and happily posed for photos with the girls.

"Are you looking forward to hearing us play tonight?" asked Craig.

"We didn't even know you were here until just now. You managed to keep that quiet," replied Sophie. "Our friends are going to be so jealous."

The boys laughed and went back to setting up for their gig.

"How on earth did you manage to book these guys with just a few weeks' notice?" Paul asked Nikki in amazement.

"Well, a few weeks ago, William and Maxine came up to the folly to sign some forms for Tom and I happened to be in the square at the time with Matt and we had a good chat with them. Turns out that Craig, the lead singer of Runners and Riders is their son, and they were more than happy to pull some strings for us," replied Nikki feeling rather proud of this achievement.

"Ah, that explains your winking earlier," said Paul catching on at last. "Well done for arranging that. In fact, you and Cleo have done an amazing job organising this wonderful party."

"You haven't seen the cost of everything yet." Nikki laughed.

This had been a bit of a strange experience for her. She and Cleo had been told to spend whatever they needed to on the party. Nikki had always been careful with money, and it felt alien to her to just spend freely. Cleo kept reassuring her that the money was coming out of the business and eventually Nikki had relaxed into the party planning process.

Constance walked over with Heather, Red and Pippa. They were all chatting happily.

"Have you enjoyed the day ladies?" asked Paul.

"It's been fabulous," enthused Red. "What a fantastic start to our life at Archer's Folly."

The rides were now illuminated with colourful neon lights and fairy lights were draped across the tops of all the other stalls. Everybody had gravitated over towards the stage and Cleo and Nikki had thoughtfully arranged for earphones to be supplied for the younger children. Runners and Riders played all their most popular songs as well as a couple of new ones from their upcoming album release. The crowd loved them and cheered joining in with the songs. Nikki had tears in her eyes feeling thrilled at how much of a success the party had been. After the concert colourful fireworks filled the sky above the folly before all the visitors started to leave. Coaches had been arranged to transport the party guests both to and from the folly to the town via Honesty, every little detail had been catered for. The clean-up operation would take place the next day, a company was coming over to the folly specifically for that purpose.

Richard and Janet had taken Ava and Riley back to their house as they were absolutely exhausted from all the excitement of the day. Everybody else wandered over to the square where the party atmosphere continued. Ollie's brother Arlo had arrived at the folly slightly later than planned. While Ollie wore his blond hair long, Arlo's was darker and had a wild unruly look. He nodded a greeting to everybody and then stood quietly next to his brother nursing a bottle of lager. Paul produced a few bottles of champagne and made sure that everybody had a glass to raise. Sophie and her friends were also allowed a glass still on an enormous high from having met and chatted with their favourite band.

"I would like to propose a toast," said Paul. "To new beginnings and new friendships. I also want to say a huge thank you to Cleo and Nikki for all the time and effort they put into planning what can only be described as the most spectacular day."

CHAPTER SEVENTEEN

Two days after the party Paul and Tom travelled up to London for a meeting with Anna before flying out to Los Angeles. Tom looked after all the legal side of Paul's work and was travelling this time as there were contracts to be signed with the film company.

Once Paul had left and the house was quiet Nikki felt a sense of calm. Everything they had all worked so hard to achieve over the last few months had culminated with a successful launch. She was excited to be teaching again and was enjoying working with the students from the local secondary schools. Nikki's art exhibition was only six weeks away now and she had finally finished her painting of the folly. Paul and the rest of the family had loved it. She had also framed Ava's painting and the little girl was thrilled when Nikki had promised that she would include it in the exhibition.

A text arrived from Cleo. *The merchandise has arrived! Have you got time to pop round?*

On my way.

They had all decided that they needed a proper logo for Archers Folly to go hand in hand with the new website.

A cup of coffee was already waiting for Nikki when she arrived at Cleo's house. It was noticeably quiet. Ava was at school and Riley was napping.

"How is Ava enjoying school?" asked Nikki.

"So far so good. It really helps that Daisy started with her. It's half days this week and then full time from next Monday. She's worn out when she gets home, though," replied Cleo.

"I had a feeling she'd like school, she's so clever I think she needed something more challenging than nursery."

"Tell me about it!" Cleo laughed. "It feels like she has been able to speak since the day I gave birth to her. Now look at the lovely merchandise that's arrived today."

They had kept the navy-blue theme that had been used in the bedrooms around the site and the new logo was a light blue cloaked archer. Nikki and Cleo started to unpack the boxes. There were t-shirts and sweatshirts for staff to wear. This would include cleaners, groundsmen, shop, and diner staff. Nikki was planning to wear them when she taught at the art castle too.

"Now what are these?" Nikki pulled out a large polythene

bag. "Brilliant, it's the flags."

There were two flags. One to go in the middle of the artisan square alongside the statue on top of the fountain. The other was to be raised above the art castle. There was also an array of pens, mugs, water bottles and notebooks.

"This all really makes the business feel nice and professional now," said Cleo.

"Definitely," agreed Nikki. "Oh, and an email arrived this morning. The BBC are coming in three weeks."

The BBC had approached Paul just after the storm. They wanted to make a documentary about Archer's Folly. They were going to interview Paul about the start of the project and to film and speak to everybody either staying or working there.

"Ooh, thanks for the heads up," said Mike as he walked in via the kitchen. "I'll get my hair and nails done."

"Maybe some Botox, too." Cleo replied laughing. "You're not getting any younger."

For the next two weeks, Nikki was busy at the art castle. As well as collaborating with the school groups she had started a folly through the seasons course. The advertising had really paid off, so much so Nikki had needed to divide the students into two groups. The idea was that they would draw and paint the folly firstly in the autumn. Then, the groups would return in the winter, spring, and summer. The Thursday session had been a group of six women who had made friends at the school gate. As they sketched and painted they chatted about their children, upcoming parties and playdates. Nikki felt sad that she would never be part of a mum's group like that.

On Friday, Nikki waited for her group to turn up at the castle. Two couples who looked to be in their sixties arrived together and were clearly all friends. They picked up the stickers with their names on and went to help themselves to cups of tea and coffee. Then a chap arrived who Nikki guessed to be in his mid to late twenties. He was covered in tattoos and piercings with a long beard into which he had plaited beads, a modern-day Viking. He wore a pair of jeans which had clearly seen better days and a T-shirt stating that archaeologists would date any old thing. Just as he was picking up his name sticker a woman walked in who looked to be in her late fifties. She wore her chestnut-coloured hair with lovely caramel highlights running through it in a smart bob cut. She wore a pair of black jeans with a cream sweatshirt.

"Hello, Miss!" exclaimed the man. He walked over and gave her a massive hug.

"Lyle Peters, how lovely to see you," replied the woman as they hugged. She was pleased to see the young man as she took the sticker showing that she was called Jo.

"I'm guessing you're a teacher, Jo?" Nikki smiled.

"How did you guess?" she asked.

"Teachers are the only people universally known as Miss or

Sir," replied Nikki.

"Miss…I mean, Jo was the best teacher I ever had," said Lyle.

"What subject do you teach?" asked Nikki.

"I taught history, but I retired last year," replied Jo. "I'm so proud of what you achieved at university Lyle," she continued.

"It was always going to be archaeology," replied Lyle. "I've been to South America, Greece and Norway on digs, and I've got you to thank for everything." He smiled at his former teacher.

Nikki thought that there was a bit of a story to be told here.

"OK, everyone, welcome to Archer's Folly," she said to the group once they had all settled with a hot drink. "So, the idea behind this group is to draw or paint the folly in the middle of our beautiful lake during each of the four seasons. Yesterday's group was incredibly lucky because we had a gloriously sunny day, and we were able to sit down at the lake with our easels. As the weather is so grotty today we have put up a large tent to protect you from the elements. I think it will be interesting to see the dramatically different pictures of the folly in the autumn. All of our equipment is already down in the tented area waiting for you so if you would like to come out to the buggy's Mike and I will drive you down to the folly."

Mike had happily volunteered his chauffeuring services as his office was so close to the castle. The group walked quickly from the buggies to the tent as the rain continued to fall heavily down from the low, grey clouds. Soon, everybody was set up and sketching away. Nikki had chatted to the two couples who said that they often signed on to different classes and courses and were also down to attend a sculpture class at the castle. Then she walked up to Jo and Lyle who were obviously thrilled to be able to catch up.

"So, tell me how Jo inspired you to become an archaeologist," said Nikki.

"Well, I'd always enjoyed history lessons at school even in the juniors," replied Lyle. "But when I went up to secondary school, life at home was really difficult. I'm one of six kids all with different dads so you can imagine how hectic life was for me. My mum didn't really have any time for us, she was always out drinking and partying."

"That must have been really hard for you," said Nikki, remembering how loving and nurturing her mother had been when she was alive.

Lyle nodded. "It really was. Two of my younger siblings got lucky and went to live with their dads. My older sister Hattie was more to like a mum than a sister. At school I joined Jo's history club and a group of archaeologists from the university came in to talk to us about how much they were learning from excavating various sites around the world and from that moment on I knew that was what I wanted to do with my life.

Jo supported me all the way."

Jo had tears in her eyes. "Lyle was such a lovely student. A lot of the other teachers had written him off because of his home environment. Statistically he was in the group who would never amount to much I'm sad to say."

"We soon proved them wrong, though," said Lyle. "I got a first in my degree and then got my masters a year later. My sister Hattie became a nurse and an exceptionally good one at that."

"That's truly amazing," said Nikki. "Jo, you must be so proud."

"Oh, I really am," replied Jo. "Incredibly proud."

"So do you fancy becoming an artist too?" asked Nikki.

"I really enjoy drawing," replied Lyle. "I often make sketches when I'm on a dig. But I was also keen to come here because I've come across some documents which imply that there could be a high-status Roman villa on the land here."

Everyone stopped what they were doing at that moment interested in what Lyle was telling them. It wasn't every day you heard about something like this so close to home.

"Oh, really? Do you know where exactly?" asked Nikki, her eyes lighting up at this news. Paul would love it too, but she hoped it wasn't on land that Paul had already built on.

"See those houses over there." Lyle pointed to where Nikki and the family lived. "Well, we think that the villa might be on the land just beyond that."

"Wow. Paul owns that land too. He'll be thrilled to think that there could be something really important still to be discovered there."

"Do you think he would let us use our ground-penetrating radar to see if there is anything worth excavating?"

"I'll be speaking to him later, he's in Los Angeles at the moment but I'll ask and then get back to you," replied Nikki. "I've a feeling he'll be incredibly keen for you to carry out your tests."

"That would be great, thank you," replied Lyle.

"If you get permission, could I come along too?" asked Jo.

"I'd be more than happy for you to come along," said Lyle. "When are you planning to go travelling though? Isn't that why you retired early?"

Jo's head dropped and they could see that she had started to cry.

Nikki put an arm around her shoulder. "Hey, what's the matter?" she asked gently.

Jo sniffed then took a tissue out of her bag. "We had big plans to travel. A Norwegian fjord cruise, the Trans-Siberia railway, Hawaii. I was really excited about it all. I just wasn't expecting to be on my own so suddenly."

"I'm so sorry for your loss, you must miss your husband every day," said Nikki, remembering the pain her family had felt when her mum had died.

Lyle took Jo's hand. He knew that Jo and her husband had never had any children of their own. "You've got me now," he said. "I'll be your family."

Jo lifted her head, looking round at the group. "No, he didn't pass away. On my last day of teaching, he told me that retirement would make him feel old. He wanted to live for the moment and be free. So, he left me and the last I heard he was living in France with a woman young enough to be his daughter," she said sadly.

One of the other women in the group gasped and frowned angrily, her eyes narrowing.

"What a pig! Sounds like you're much better off without him," she said.

"We were married for twenty-five years, so it came as a bit of a shock to find out that I didn't really know him at all," said Jo. "But now I've recovered from it all I'm determined to live my very best life too."

"Good for you," the woman replied walking over and giving Jo a big hug.

At the end of the course Mike had driven the two couples back up to the castle leaving Lyle and Jo chatting to Nikki while she tidied up. Lyle had presented her with a card bearing his contact details.

"Would you want to wait until next spring to carry out your

testing?" Jo asked.

"No, my team would be up here as soon as we possibly could. If we found anything worth excavating I'd need to put in an application to the university for funding. In which case it would probably be next year before we could start the actual dig," replied Lyle. He fished his phone out of his pocket and swiped until he found the photos he had taken of the documents.

"If you both give me your phone numbers, I'll send over what I've found. It'll be some nice light reading for you."

"Paul would be very interested in reading all this," replied Nikki, looking forward to telling him all about it and forwarding on the documents. This would be right up his street.

"Thanks," replied Jo, her eyes sparkling at the prospect of getting involved. "This is all very exciting. It's been over twenty years since I last went on a dig, I used to go during the school holidays. I can't wait to get my hands dirty again."

Later that evening Paul video called Nikki. "Are you missing me?" he asked, feeling homesick as soon as he saw her face.

"I am," she replied. "I need you to keep my feet warm in bed at night."

"Very funny! Well, the good news is that we'll be finishing here today. We're booked onto a flight tonight so we'll be back at the folly by lunchtime," said Paul smiling when he saw Nikki's face light up at the news.

Nikki beamed. "I can't wait to see you! I wasn't expecting you back until next week. I'll cook a nice romantic dinner for us tomorrow. Anyway, I found out something interesting from one of my students today."

"Intriguing, do tell," replied Paul.

"Lyle works as an archaeologist for Kent University, and he's come across some old documents that suggest that there might be a high-status Roman villa on the land adjacent to our houses. He wanted me to ask you for permission to carry out some ground-penetrating radar tests to see if there is any credence to what he has read," Nikki said, already knowing how Paul would react.

Paul eyes lit up. "High status, eh? That would be fantastic! Of course, he has my permission."

"I had a feeling you'd say that. I'll send you the photos of the documents that Lyle has found. If they find anything then they'll apply for the funding from the university for the project so that they can start the excavation next year."

"Tell him that I'll fund the project, the university's funds are probably quite limited. That way he can keep going for as long as it takes."

"Paul Archer, you are the kindest, loveliest man I have ever known," said Nikki. "I can't wait for you to come home."

"There'll be no more trips to the Los Angeles after this one. I love you, Nikki," he said softly.

"I love you too," she replied, and they ended the call.

Nikki called Lyle straight away. "Paul is ecstatic to hear about the prospect of a Roman villa and is more than happy for you to go ahead with the project. Also, he would like to fund the whole project to enable you to work for as long as you need to," she said.

"That's fantastic news. I'm looking forward to meeting Paul," replied Lyle. "My team will be delighted. Jo has offered to let me stay with her in Honesty, I think she could do with the company, and I certainly don't mind moving out of the room I'm renting."

"By the sound of it, you've turned up at exactly the right time for Jo. I felt sorry for her today, but this will give her a new focus. Plus, she seems to be very fond of you."

"I honestly owe her a lot. If she hadn't believed in me I wouldn't be talking to you today that's for sure," replied Lyle.

"We shall look forward to meeting you and your team soon," said Nikki as she ended the call.

Nikki was so excited at the prospect of Paul returning home that she could hardly sleep. She dashed out the next morning to buy everything she needed to cook a lovely romantic meal for them.

When Paul buzzed to come in the gates Nikki dashed to

open the front door desperate to close the space between them and to hug him tightly. She flew at him as soon as he got out of his car.

"I'll have to go away more often if this is the greeting I get." Paul laughed in between the kisses Nikki was showering on him.

"I've really missed you."

"Want to show me how much?" he murmured in her ear.

They had dozed off in each other's arms after some energetic lovemaking. Nikki woke up and pulled the duvet back having checked the time. She needed to get on with the Beef Wellington she had planned to make for dinner. It was Paul's favourite.

"Where are you going?" he asked sleepily.

"I'm going to make a start on the special dinner I promised you," Nikki replied as she leaned over to kiss him.

He pulled her back down. "Make it tomorrow," he said. "I need you here."

Unable to resist Nikki rolled on top of Paul. "Here I am," she whispered. "I'll always be here for you."

CHAPTER EIGHTEEN

The BBC arrived in force ready to make the documentary about the folly. It had been arranged that while the film crew conducted some initial filming around the site, Karen Donohue a much-loved tv presenter would interview Paul and the family at his house. After all the introductions had been made the interview began.

"So, Paul, I've had a good look round this morning, and I must ask where on earth all the ideas came from for the different areas of the folly?" Karen asked.

Everyone laughed at that, they had asked Paul the same question a million times.

"In the world we live in we have our phones, computers and other distractions. I just wanted to create somewhere where writers and artists could go off-grid either for inspiration or just to carry out their craft in peace," began Paul.

"I love the fairy tale cottages," agreed Karen.

"We wanted to install buildings for writers and artists retreats and residential courses. It made sense for the writers building to be built in a Tudor style as a homage to William Shakespeare."

"I get that," said Karen. "But what about the Bavarian castle?"

"I saw many castles in that style when I was in Germany. They're so beautiful and when I was planning the folly it just came to me in a flash. Of course, it's just the frontage, inside we have ultramodern facilities which are being used by local schools and for the courses run by my partner Nikki," replied Paul.

Nikki blushed, unused to being the centre of attention. "We also employ potter's and sculptors to run courses here," she squeaked and got a surreptitious nudge from Paul in response.

"I think it's brilliant you're allowing schools to take advantage of the facilities that you have here. Especially in a time when there are so many budget cuts being made," said Karen, looking impressed.

"I'm lucky enough to have made a good living from my writing and I'm more than happy to give back and offer students the chance to flourish," said Paul.

"And then of course, we must talk about the artisan square," Karen continued. "Where did that idea come from?"

"It saddens me that we're starting to lose the high streets around the country as people move to ordering items online. For those who try to persevere with running a shop they're finding the rents too high to make their business workable. I'm worried that traditional arts and crafts will lose their way and I wanted to create a space where artisans could practise, teach, and sell their craft. Our units are affordable, the tenants are more than happy to show visitors from the public and schools what they do. We'll be having open day's once a month where they can sell the items that they make in the shops at the entrance to the square. They will also be selling online which, much as it pains me to see retail going that way, our craftspeople do have a living to make. Of course, a lot of my books are sold online too, so it would be hypocritical of me to slam the digital markets," replied Paul.

"Which answers what was going to be my next question," said Karen, striking a line through her notes. "You're just trying to preserve traditional crafts and face to face sales."

"Exactly right."

"You've told me about Nikki and how she teaches at the castle. I can see that this is very much a family affair. What does everybody else do?"

"I'm Mike and I'm Paul and Tom's cousin. This is my wife Cleo. I'm the general manager here, so all the contractors have reported into me during the construction phase. Now I'll be here for the day to day running plus any future development work. Cleo is an interior designer and she helped us a lot with everything."

"I'm Tom and I'm the family lawyer. I look after all of Paul's contracts for his books, movie deals and everything to do with the folly."

Karen nodded. "At this point I would like to tell any viewers that didn't already know, Paul Archer writes bestselling thrillers. The Denver File which is the current movie on screens worldwide now was based on his novel and I believe that this week Hollywood has signed up another one of your books."

"That's right, Karen, Tom and I have recently returned from Los Angeles to sign the contracts relating to The Royal Spy being made into a movie. It's all extremely exciting," said Paul.

"That's brilliant," said Karen. "Let's continue with the introductions."

"I'm Richard and this is my wife Janet. We're Paul's parents. I look after health and safety and Janet looks after the human resources."

"So, do you have any other plans to build here?" asked Karen.

"Well, we have an archaeology team scanning the land next to us here as they think that there might be a high-status

Roman villa waiting to be excavated and I'm extremely excited about that. We're also drawing up some plans with the aim to build a retirement village and respite centre for people stuck in their homes with their carer's. We want to give others the opportunity to enjoy the tranquillity here," said Paul.

"How exciting!" said Karen. "And what a lovely gesture."

"It was Nikki's idea really," said Paul as Nikki blushed once again. "But a good one."

"Big thanks to you all for taking the time to speak to me," said Karen. "Now we're going to be speaking to everybody else who lives here at Archers Folly."

With the camera now off, Karen hugged them all while Mike got ready to drive both her and the camera operator down to the artisan square.

"I think that went well," said Janet once the crew had left the house.

"Me too," replied Paul. "I'm sure the people down in the square will have lots of good things to say too."

"I think I might go down there myself," said Tom.

"Any particular reason why?" Paul grinned. "Would it be anything to do with a certain young lady called Heather?"

Now it was Tom's turn to blush. "No, not at all. Just thought I should be around in case any questions were asked that they might not have an answer for."

"If that's your reason for going down there then fill your

boots." Paul laughed.

"Leave the lad alone," said Janet. "What's wrong if he did have a bit of a liking for Heather, she seems like a lovely young lady."

Tom just sighed and left the house. The thing is, they had all hit the nail on the head. He couldn't stop thinking about Heather. She was pretty and her shyness captivated him. He had seen her more relaxed side at the opening party and when she had laughed her whole face had just lit up.

Karen and her team had now set up in the artisan square and first she headed for Mitch and Mabel's unit. She spoke to the camera, "Mitch and Mabel are becoming a household name in the home fragrance sector. Their candles and reed diffusers are selling as fast as their competitors. Let's go inside and have a chat with them." Karen took in the lovely fragrances filling the air in the unit as Mitch and Mabel walked towards her.

"Welcome to Mitch and Mabel." Mabel grinned. This was great publicity for them.

"This place smells divine," said Karen. "What are you working on here?"

"We're working on some new fragrances for our spring and summer range," said Mitch. "Christmas was all done and dusted months ago and now we're looking forward to getting our new range out to the shops in time for the spring and summer season."

"What fragrances are you creating out here?" asked Karen while gesturing to her camera operator to take a sweeping shot of the workshop. Mitch shook his head and put his body between him and the camera.

"All secrets here," he said. "You'll have to wait until next year to find out."

"What do you think about life here at Archers Folly?" asked Karen.

"We love it here," said Mabel. "It's quiet and has a great creative vibe. Living and working next door to other creative people is a dream come true."

"I second that," said Mitch, putting his arm around his wife.

"Well, thank you for your time," said Karen. "It's time to go next door and introduce ourselves."

Red was impatiently waiting for it to be her turn. She was dressed in her usual land girl garb this time in purple dungarees with a matching headscarf. She motioned for Pippa to come over too. Karen looked at her notes and then walked over to them.

"Hello, ladies. Please introduce yourselves to the camera," she said.

"My name's Pippa and this is my wife Red," said Pippa. "We met at a Lindy Hop competition in Las Vegas sixteen years ago. Red's from New York and she moved over to live with me in the UK shortly after that. We're happily married now."

"I love Lindy Hop dancing!" exclaimed Karen. "I've had a go and it really keeps you fit."

"For sure, we love it," replied Red. "So, we've taken over two units here. I upcycle furniture, I hate to see anything just chucked away. Pippa makes vintage style clothing."

Karen looked admiringly at their outfits. Pippa was wearing a beautiful blue full circle dress covered in white polka dots.

"You're both very stylish," said Karen. "I wish you the very best of luck here at Archer's Folly."

The BBC team walked over to Constance's unit where she was busy working on an intricate flower display.

"Hi," said Karen. "Have you got a minute to chat to us please?"

"Of course," said Constance standing up and walking across to join Karen and her team.

Karen looked at the display Constance had been working on. There were fragrant flowers, grasses, ribbons, and crystals all weaved in together.

"This is pretty amazing," said Karen admiring the intricate work.

"Thank you so much," replied Constance with a smile. "This display is going into the reception of a luxury hotel down in Dorset."

"How wonderful," replied Karen. "And how are enjoying life here at the folly?"

"I've known Paul Archer for a number of years and as soon as he told me about his plans, I put my name down for a unit straight away. This is such a lovely peaceful environment to work in, such a change from my old shop on a busy road in London," Constance replied.

"The peace, tranquillity, and creativity seem to be the overriding reasons for everybody coming to work here," said Karen.

"Absolutely," agreed Constance. "This is a wonderful place to work in."

Next, Karen tapped on the door to Heather's unit, which, unlike the other units was closed. Heather looked up from her work, seemingly startled by the arrival of the documentary team. She looked over Karen's shoulder and saw Tom standing just outside and he nodded reassuringly.

"Hi, Heather, I'm Karen from the BBC. Could you spare me a moment to talk about this lovely silver jewellery that you're making here?" she asked.

Reluctantly, Heather stood up. "I love to make very thin and intricate pieces. I'm working on a silver spider's web design for a necklace that could be worn with some pretty evening dresses."

"It's really beautiful," said Karen, bending over to admire

the work. "Are you missing life up in Scotland?"

Heather shook her head. "Not really. I saw this place advertised in a magazine and I thought it would be a good place to set up properly. I always worked in my Dad's garage before that."

Heather saw Tom give her a thumbs up and she caught his eye and gave him a lovely smile. He waited until Karen and her camera operator had moved on to William and Maxine and he walked in to speak to her.

"Sorry about the intrusion. Paul thought that agreeing to this documentary would be great publicity for you all," he said apologetically.

"Oh! I don't mind really," replied Heather. "I'm just not a very chatty person."

Tom also admired the spider's web design that Heather was working on.

"This is really very clever. You've got real talent, Heather," he said.

She blushed before returning to her seat. "It's sweet of you to say so. I love trying out new and unique designs."

Karen and her team visited the other businesses before finally arriving to speak to James. He was working on a box made up of different coloured varnished woods. There were drawers fitted all around the box which were different in size and depths.

"What's this you're working on?" asked Karen, noting several similar boxes on the shelves around the workshop.

"This is one of my best sellers," said James proudly. "It's a wooden advent calendar. If you look closely you can see that I have engraved numbers on each drawer. It can be reused every year and even passed down to other family members as they come along. I've made the drawers in assorted sizes to allow for different advent gifts to go inside."

"What a wonderful and sustainable idea!" said Karen "I love it. I can see why these sell so well. After this programme goes out you'll be inundated with orders."

James laughed. "Thank you so much. My order book is actually full for this Christmas now, but I would advise people to get in early with their orders for next year because these do take quite a bit of time to make," he said blushing. He had led a very quiet life looking after his mother until she had died. This was a new and exciting phase of his life.

"But look at the fantastic quality. I can see why you've received so many orders. And are you enjoying working here at the folly?" asked Karen.

"I love it here; I've made some good friends and it's a wonderful place to work in," replied James.

Once Karen and her team had finished in the square, they finally made their way to the diner for a well-deserved lunch.

Tom returned to Paul and Nikki's house where he found

them hard at work in the garden. Nikki had asked if Paul would mind her trying to create a colourful space just like her mother had done. Paul had thought that this was a great idea and was eager to learn about gardening himself. He had found it to be surprisingly therapeutic. They were busy planting bulbs and winter bedding plants into wooden troughs. Nikki had already planted the cuttings she had taken from her mum's garden.

"Hi," said Tom. "Just letting you know Karen and her team have finished their interviews and the last I saw of them they were headed to the diner."

"That's good. I should imagine she would have heard lots of pleasant things from our new tenants," said Paul as he poured some soil into one of the troughs.

"You're absolutely right there. It was also great publicity for them all," replied Tom, impressed at the work Paul and Nikki were doing to their garden. "Did she give you any idea when the show was going to be broadcast?"

"I have a feeling that it could be as early as next week. Karen said that she would email me to let me know of the exact date," replied Paul.

"We'll have to organise an open day for the following weekend then," said Nikki as she took a long drink from her water bottle. "People will be keen to come and have a look after they have seen the programme."

"I'll get Dad and Mike on the case," said Paul as he reached over to the tray containing the bedding plants they had bought from the nearby nursery. "Nikki and I will be busy getting ready for her art exhibition in Cambridge."

"Of course, I'd forgotten about that," said Tom. "Well, the garden is coming on nicely, you can do mine afterwards if you like."

"Very funny, do it yourself. You could do with the exercise," replied Paul. He was thoroughly enjoying creating a garden with Nikki.

Nikki loved hearing the banter between the brothers. She shivered in anticipation. Her exhibition was just two weeks away. The gallery owners, her university friend Scarlet and her husband Alex had been publicising the exhibition on the local radio and newspaper as well as online. She was incredibly grateful for this opportunity to display her work. The exhibition had been years in the making bridging her marriage to Harry and now her relationship with Paul. Hopefully, it would be successful.

CHAPTER NINETEEN

The day before Nikki's art exhibition Paul picked up a rental van. Each painting had been very carefully bubble wrapped and they ensured that there was adequate padding in between each frame. Finally, they made sure that nothing could move while they were driving to Cambridge.

Nikki felt tired, she hadn't slept well at all over the last few nights. Paul looked across at her, frowning.

"Are you feeling OK, Nikki?" he asked, noticing her pale face with dark rings under her eyes. He hoped she hadn't overworked herself with her teaching at the art castle as well as preparing for her exhibition.

She nodded. "I'm fine. This exhibition is so important for me, I just hope that plenty of people come along. I'd hate it if the gallery stayed empty all day."

"Hey, you mustn't worry," Paul replied. "You said that

Scarlet and Alex had run an advertising campaign. I'm sure people will come along to look at your art."

Nikki exhaled. "I really hope that they do." She giggled. "Wasn't Ava excited to see her painting of the folly in its frame?"

Paul smiled. "You've been so kind spending time with Ava. I know Cleo really appreciates the time and effort you've given her," he said.

"It's been an absolute pleasure. Ava will undoubtedly have an exhibition of her own one day," Nikki replied.

The plan was that the rest of the family would travel to Cambridge the next day. The exhibition was due to open at noon. Once Ava had seen her painting on display and the adults had looked at Nikki's artwork, they were all going with the children to the Corn Exchange to see the pantomime.

Nikki phoned her friends as soon as they got close to the gallery, and they were waiting at the back ready to guide Paul as he reversed the van into their yard.

"Nikki, how lovely to see you again!" said Scarlet giving her a welcoming hug. "It feels like ages since we last got together."

"We've been really busy at the folly," replied Nikki. "And I'm teaching again which feels fantastic." She looked across at Paul. "I'm so sorry, where are my manners. Scarlet, Alex, this is my partner, Paul Archer."

Alex shook Paul's hand and then looked across at the van.

"OK, let's get your paintings in and set up. I'm really looking forward to seeing them all."

Paul and Alex carried the paintings in while Nikki followed Scarlet upstairs to the flat above the gallery to put their overnight bag in the guest bedroom. A little while later Alex appeared at the doorway.

"Nikki, would you like to come down and show us how you would like the paintings arranged?" he asked.

"Oh, yes, I do have a plan in my head about how I'd like them displayed," Nikki replied, putting her cup onto the coffee table and standing up.

Most of her paintings were of the Kent countryside, she had painted them while she had been married to Harry. But her two favourites were the paintings depicting the beautiful garden that her mum had created. She felt a lump in her throat as she looked at them. Now that Chris had sold the house, apart from a few photos, this was the only real reminder she had left of the garden.

Paul gave her a hug. "Happy memories though."

"Oh, most definitely," she replied.

They placed the painting of the folly in the centre of the display. It was the largest painting and Paul thought it was Nikki's best. They put Ava's much smaller painting next to it.

Alex walked out with another frame. "I'm a bit confused about this one." He turned it round to show them.

It was the painting of the serious-looking gentleman sitting at his large desk that Nikki had rescued from Chris's loft.

"Oh, I didn't mean to bring that with me, I must have packed it by mistake. It was something that my dad bought at a jumble sale years ago for fifty pence. My mum hated it, so it was put up in the loft until I cleared it out a few months ago. I was planning to clean it up a bit when I finally got some time," Nikki said.

"Fifty pence!" exclaimed Alex. "That's unbelievable!"

"Why?"

"In the eighteen seventies, Sir Leonard Gill painted a dozen portraits under the collective name of *The captains of Industry* About ten years ago the collection was brought together for an exhibition, but one was missing. I have a feeling that this is the missing portrait and not a copy. If I'm right then this is Lord Gerald Tolly, he owned a large, successful shipping company. Nikki this is potentially worth a small fortune. I can't believe that your dad bought it at a jumble sale for fifty pence," said Alex his eyes wide open in surprise at this discovery.

"Incredible!" said Nikki in amazement. "Dad will be blown away."

"Would you allow me to clean it up and carry out some restoration work?" asked Alex. He was thrilled to have the opportunity to restore the painting to its former glory.

"I'd be more than happy to let you restore it, I honestly

don't have any time at all at the moment," replied Nikki. "Thank you so much."

"This is an extremely exciting find; I can't wait to get cracking. It'll look magnificent when it's all cleaned up and we should see all of the nuances that made Gill one of our finest artists," said Alex looking flushed with the excitement of potentially revealing a lost painting by a renowned artist had been found to the art world

Once the gallery was all ready for the opening they went for a walk along the side of the river Cam. It was a sunny winters day, and they were all wrapped up warmly. Nikki and Paul walked along hand in hand.

"Happy?" Paul asked Nikki.

She gazed at him with her beautiful, clear green eyes, full of love for him.

"I can honestly say that this is the happiest I've ever been," she replied.

That evening Nikki insisted on treating Scarlet and Alex to dinner. She felt that it was the least she could do to thank them for arranging the exhibition for her. They ate at a bistro which served traditional British food.

"We saw the documentary about your folly last night," said Scarlet. "It looks like an amazing place."

"It really is," said Nikki. "You must visit us soon. Although I must warn you that once you arrive you'll never want to leave."

Paul looked thoughtful. "You know, if you ever decide to move out of Cambridge, we could always build a gallery for you to work out of. It would fit perfectly with the creative environment," he said.

Alex took a sip of his wine, then glanced sideways at Scarlet who smiled back at him.

"Well, if the council keeps putting the rent up here then we might just take you up on that offer," he replied.

Nikki felt excited. As usual her mind started to buzz with ideas. "It would be great if you moved to the folly. Now you really must visit soon."

When the doors to the gallery were opened the following day, Nikki was relieved to see several people walking in. Scarlet had employed two waiting staff to serve champagne, orange juice and canapes to their guests. It wasn't too long before they heard Ava's excited voice.

"Hi, everyone." Paul picked the little girl up. "Ava, do you want to have a look at your painting?"

"Yes please," said Ava. She had been warned by Cleo that if she didn't behave herself she wouldn't be going to the pantomime. She watched as a man placed an orange sticker on the frame of Nikki's painting of the folly.

"What's that sticker for?"

"It means that I want to buy this wonderful painting," said

the man, smiling at her.

"Do you like my painting too?" asked Ava.

The man studied her painting for a moment then turned back to Ava. "You are a very talented young lady." As he spoke to Ava, Alex walked up to her painting and put a sticker on the frame.

"Look, Nikki! Someone wants to buy my painting," she said joyfully.

"I knew somebody would buy it," said Nikki winking at Richard and Janet who had every intention of putting the painting on the wall of their living room. Chris looked misty-eyed when he studied the paintings of his former garden. "I love these, you've captured everything your mum created," he said choking up.

Nikki hugged him, tearful herself. "Thanks, Dad. That means a lot," she replied.

The rest of the family disappeared off to enjoy the pantomime and slowly the number of visitors at the gallery dwindled. Nikki had sold every painting, she was overwhelmed. Finally, there was just one visitor left, an elegant looking woman who had clearly had a lot of cosmetic work conducted on her smooth face. Her hair was a beautiful snowy white.

"Hi, Nikki," she said in an accent not dissimilar to Red's New York drawl but more refined.

"My name is Julia Unwin, I own galleries in New York, Chicago and Miami. I've been in the UK for the past month visiting exhibitions like yours. I'm extremely impressed with your work. Your paintings are so clear and alive, they could almost be mistaken for photographs. I would love you to come over to the USA next year to display some more of your art," she said as she handed Nikki a black and gold embossed business card.

"Thank you so much," she replied, stunned with this sudden turn of events. "Unfortunately, I'm terribly busy now, and I don't have as much time to paint as I used to. But thank you for your kind offer."

"Well, the invitation's always there my dear and congratulations on this wonderful exhibition," said Julia before she left the gallery.

Paul frowned at Nikki in surprise. "What a tremendous opportunity this is for you. Surely you could make some time to paint. I'd hate to think that you were missing the chance to exhibit your art around the world because of your commitments at the folly."

"Honestly, its fine. I'm loving my life right now and it took me years to paint everything you see here. Maybe in the future, who knows?" Nikki replied.

As they got ready to leave Nikki hugged Scarlet. "Thank you for today, it's been terrific," she said.

"You're welcome," replied her friend. "I knew your paintings would sell, and what an honour for Julia Unwin to approach you too. I didn't even know she was here in the UK," Scarlet replied.

"Please come and visit us soon," said Nikki.

"We'll definitely be visiting you after Christmas," said Alex, looking knowingly at Paul. "And of course, I'll keep you up to speed with the Leonard Gill painting."

A few hours they arrived back at home.

"Why don't you go upstairs and run yourself a bath and I'll make something for us to eat," suggested Paul.

Nikki felt exhausted. Her legs ached and she had the thumping start of a headache too. She rubbed her temple, the thought of a lovely, scented bath really appealing to her.

"That sounds like a good plan to me," she replied gratefully, feeling lucky at having such a kind and considerate partner.

A little while later she went downstairs and was blown away at the sight that greeted her. Paul had lit dozens of candles creating a romantic setting. There were coloured fairy lights hanging around the doors and windows. Her favourite Ed Sheeran song was playing. He walked towards Nikki and handed her a glass of champagne. She was touched that Paul had gone to such a lot of trouble to celebrate her exhibition. He cleared his throat.

"Nikki, I love you so much, you make me incredibly happy. I know that I've found my soul mate," he said with tears glistening in his eyes.

Nikki's eyes welled up, too.

Paul knelt in front of her presenting a box from Tiffany holding the most beautiful ring she had ever seen. It had a large princess cut diamond set in a platinum band which was also set with diamonds. "Nikki Pembroke, will you marry me?"

Nikki took the ring from Paul and slipped it onto her finger. "Of course, I'll marry you. There's nothing I want more than to be your wife you lovely, gorgeous man."

They sat at the dining table where Paul served up a creamy chicken pasta dish. Nikki kept moving her hand around admiring the reflection of the diamonds from the pretty lighting around the room.

"I take it you like the ring," said Paul, pleased to see that he had made the right choice. He had told Cleo of his plans and when he showed her the ring she had nodded in approval.

"I absolutely love it!" Nikki beamed.

"So, I was thinking about the wedding," said Paul. "I thought that perhaps we could get married in June over by the lake. We could put up a floral gazebo with white chairs for our guests and a marquee for the reception. What do you think?"

"I think that's a wonderful idea," said Nikki smiling. "But we're going to be very busy in June so we should rethink the date."

Paul felt a brief feeling of irritation but quickly pushed it away. He knew Nikki's intentions were well placed.

"Nikki darling, today I heard you turn down the opportunity to display your artwork over in America because of your commitments to the folly. Now you're suggesting that we'll be too busy to get married. Nothing is in the diary yet for next summer, surely? If there is, then we'll move things around to accommodate our wedding."

Nikki looked straight into Paul's eyes. "We're both going to be too busy to get married in June because that's around the time that our baby is going to be born." For a moment Nikki thought that Paul was going to drop his glass onto the table. She had left her champagne untouched. "Say that again," said Paul with an incredulous look on his face.

"I'm pregnant and by my calculations our baby will be due in June," Nikki said, almost as shocked at the news herself.

Paul stood up and walked round the table where he picked Nikki up and carefully swung her round. "I'm going to be a dad!" He grinned. "When did you carry out the test?"

"*Tests*," replied Nikki. "Lots of them. I got up early this morning because I wanted to know. I was so sure that I couldn't get pregnant. But I'd been feeling so tired over the last couple of weeks, and I was overdue, so I did the tests and, well, here we are. I suspect that we conceived the day you returned from Los Angeles."

"You don't know how happy you've made me," he said, kissing her.

"If it's OK with you, I'd like to keep this news to ourselves until we after the first scan. I just don't want to jinx anything," said Nikki, rubbing her hands on her face. "I'm as excited as you but I'm also quite scared."

"I understand," said Paul, unable to keep the grin from his face. "What a wonderful secret to keep though."

Nikki was looking out of the window at the garden when she suddenly had a thought.

"I've got an idea about the wedding. How would you feel if we got married here in our garden on Christmas Eve? I'd feel like Mum was here with us and we could keep it nice and intimate with just family and a few friends. Unless you really wanted something larger that is?"

"Nikki, I think that would be perfect," replied Paul. "Let's invite everyone round tomorrow and tell them our news."

The following afternoon, everybody arrived at the house and Paul set up a zoom call with his sister Ruth who was working with Medecins Sans Frontieres in Brazil as a doctor. Nikki had spoken to her a few times over the previous months and liked her. She was very driven in her humanitarian work.

Paul handed out champagne to everybody with juice for Ava and Riley. Nikki took her champagne as she didn't want to draw attention to herself by having juice. She had no intention of drinking a single drop though. Paul tapped on his glass to get everybody's attention.

"The other day I asked Chris for Nikki's hand in marriage. He happily agreed knowing what an excellent catch I am. I proposed to Nikki last night when we got home from her remarkably successful exhibition and she accepted," he said

Everyone cheered and Nikki dutifully held out her hand to show off her new engagement ring. Paul put his arm around Nikki's shoulder.

"We've decided that we would like to get married in a small ceremony here in our garden on Christmas Eve. Just for the family and some close friends," said Paul.

"What a nice idea," said Janet warmly. "I love it."

"Santa can come to the wedding too," said Ava jumping up and down in excitement. Riley joined in jumping next to his sister.

"Santa! Santa!" they shouted.

"OK, you two, stop shouting please," instructed Mike and they quietened down at once although they couldn't stop the smiles and they kept nudging each other.

"Ruth, will you be coming home this Christmas?" asked Tom. Ruth hadn't been home for the past three Christmases.

She pulled a face. "I'm so sorry everyone but we're really up against it with another strain of the virulent sickness bug we've been fighting for the past eighteen months. We've lost some staff recently and we're working around the clock. I promise to get home as soon as we can break this horrible infection cycle," she said shaking her head sadly.

Everybody knew how hard Ruth worked and Janet worried about her all the time. Her face always looked so strained and tired whenever they had a video call.

"We understand," said Nikki. "Perhaps you could come to the wedding in the same way you joined our engagement party today."

Ruth nodded. "I will do my utmost to be part of the wedding. My baby brother is finally settling down and with such a lovely lady too," she said.

She looked away and spoke to someone at her end and then turned to face the family again. "Well, duty calls again. Congratulations, guys, see you all soon. Love you," Ruth said before ending the call.

"How about your brother and sister, Nikki, have you told them the good news?" asked Janet.

Nikki and Chris exchanged a look. "Oh yes," said Nikki. "I messaged them both last night and all I got back was a thumbs up emoji from Jess and nothing from Stuart."

Chris sighed. "I'm afraid that's so typical of those two I'm sorry to say," he spoke with sadness in his voice.

"Oh, what a shame," said Janet, feeling sorry for them. She

couldn't even begin to imagine what it would be like if her own family was as fractured as Chris and Nikki's.

"It's fine," replied Chris knowing that it wasn't fine at all. "We're used to it now."

Just then Nikki's phone rang. She saw that it was Lyle calling. "Hi, Lyle," she greeted him.

"Hi, Nikki, is Paul with you by any chance? I've got some big news for you both," he asked.

"As it happens, the whole family is right here. Paul and I have just got engaged," replied Nikki.

"Congratulations to you both. As you're otherwise engaged, excuse the pun, I'll call back tomorrow," said Lyle.

"No, let me put you on speakerphone, big news can't wait," said Nikki, keen to know the outcome of Lyle's investigative geophysical scans.

Nikki spoke to the room. "It's our archaeologist Lyle, he's got some news for us all. Lyle, we're all listening."

Lyle cleared his throat. "Well, on Thursday we did a survey of the land we had identified as a possible Roman site using ground-penetrating radar. We've reviewed the results and there is evidence of either a very high-status villa or possibly a Roman palace. There are lots of buildings and they even appear to continue into the field beyond too," he said rushing his words in his excitement.

"That's tremendous news Lyle," said Paul. "As I mentioned

previously I'd like to fully fund the dig. We'll get together next week to iron out the details, but I want you to have all of the state-of-the-art equipment that you'd need for the excavation."

"That's a really generous offer Paul which I accept wholeheartedly. OK, let's speak next week and produce a proper plan of action. I think it would take at least two years to fully excavate the site. And congratulations to you and Nikki once again," Lyle replied.

The call ended with Paul looking like the cat that got the cream.

"All good news seems to come in threes," he said suddenly noticing that Nikki was fixing him with an icy stare.

"Three pieces of good news?" queried Cleo raising an eyebrow.

"Absolutely, firstly Nikki's exhibition was an enormous success and she's been invited to display her work in the States whenever she is ready to do so. We've got engaged and now we potentially have a Roman palace on our land," Paul said.

"Nice save," whispered Nikki shortly afterwards.

Paul looked apologetic. "Yeah sorry about that, I can't wait until we can tell everybody our other good news,"

"Me neither, but you understand my reasoning though?" Nikki frowned

"Of course, I do. But I'm sure everything will be fine," Paul replied.

What a weekend.. A successful exhibition, the potential discovery of a long-lost portrait, Paul's surprise proposal. Nikki thought.

She placed her hands over her tummy. "But you are the best piece of news ever," she whispered to her baby.

CHAPTER TWENTY

First thing the next morning, Nikki rang the registry office and spoke to a lovely registrar called Summer Hopkins. She lived in Honesty and had visited the folly on its open day and was more than happy to marry Paul and Nikki at their home even though it was officially her day off.

"That's so kind of you, Summer," said Nikki warmly. It had been a big ask to get somebody to conduct the ceremony on Christmas Eve.

"It's my pleasure," Summer replied. "I'm a sucker for romance, it's why I do the job I do."

Later, Cleo and Nikki walked down to the square. They wanted to speak to William and Maxine about invitations and Connie about the wedding flowers.

"Where do you want to get your wedding dress from?" asked Cleo.

"Well, when I married Harry I had the full white wedding, and I don't want to do that again. I was thinking about asking Pippa if she would have enough time to make me something more vintage to wear. I also want Ava to be a bridesmaid so we would need to get a dress for her too," replied Nikki.

"Ava would love that," said Cleo, smiling at how Ava would react to the news.

"I want to find out if anybody is staying here over Christmas because they will of course be invited to the wedding," said Nikki as they walked through Mitch and Mabel's door.

"Did I hear you mention a wedding as you walked in?" asked Mabel.

"We most certainly did," said Nikki. "We got engaged over the weekend and we're planning to get married in our garden on Christmas Eve. Will you be staying here for Christmas? If so you're invited."

"We're staying put this year," replied Mabel. "We would love to come along."

"Would Daisy like to be a bridesmaid with Ava?" Nikki asked.

"She would be thrilled to be a bridesmaid," replied Mabel.

Mitch beamed. "She was quite upset back in the summer because one of her cousins was a bridesmaid and she asked us why she couldn't be one. This will be a great Christmas present for her," he said.

They almost bumped into Jabulani as they walked back out into the square.

"Hi Jabulani, we were just wondering what your plans were for Christmas? It's just that Paul and I are getting married on Christmas Eve and you're more than welcome to come along," asked Nikki.

"Congratulations," replied Jabulani. "We won't be here over Christmas and the New Year; we're going to Wales to stay with Fearne's sister. But thank you for the invitation."

"No problem," replied Nikki. "Fearne must be so happy to be spending the holiday with her sister after all this time."

"She's really happy," replied Jabulani. "As am I,"

William and Maxine were also delighted with the news of Nikki and Paul's upcoming wedding. "You're just in time," said Maxine when Nikki had asked them to produce the wedding invitations. "We're off to Canada for a month next week so you'll be our very last order before we fly."

Connie was more than happy to supply the flowers for the wedding.

"We would need a nice winter flower bouquet for myself and posies for the two bridesmaids. Buttonholes and corsages for the guests, we're not having a lot of guests given the date.

I'm sure most people will be at home preparing for their own Christmases," said Nikki.

"Oh, and if possible I was thinking about having a pergola draped with winter flowers too as we are having the wedding ceremony in the garden, weather permitting," said Nikki.

"No problem, and please consider the flowers as my gift to you both," replied Connie, who was travelling home on the morning of Christmas Eve to spend the holiday with her family.

Nikki was feeling really excited now. Things were starting to come together very quickly. She was disappointed to discover that Red and Pippa were away for the next two days as they were taking part in a Lindy Hop competition in Manchester, but she had sent Pippa a text requesting a chat about her wedding dress. She had received a happy text of congratulations in return.

It turned out that everyone was going elsewhere for Christmas except for Mitch, Mabel, and James.

"I would love to come along to your wedding, what an exciting day to get married. Richard and Janet have already invited me to join them on Christmas day," said James.

James had become a member of their friendship group when one evening he had been enjoying a pint in the pub on quiz night. Richard had recognised him and invited him to join their team. It turned out that he was a deeply knowledgeable man and they had won the quiz easily with his contribution. He was now a regular member of the team.

"That all went well," said Cleo as they walked back home. "I hope Riley's behaved himself with Janet this morning."

Riley was now an official member of the terrible two's club and was throwing regular tantrums. Cleo was finding it utterly exhausting and had found herself snapping at Mike a lot which was very out of character for her.

As Nikki let herself into the house, Lyle was just finishing his meeting with Paul.

"Did the planning all go well guys?" she asked guessing that it had from their happy-looking faces.

"Definitely," said Paul. "The project will start in the spring. Lyle is going to leave his job at the university and work for us instead. That will give him the freedom that he needs to concentrate on the excavation."

The men shook hands. "I'm looking forward to getting started," said Lyle.

Once Lyle had left Paul gave Nikki a hug. "How did your morning go?" he asked.

She spun round to face him her eyes lighting up with excitement. "Connie is going to provide the flowers as her gift to us which is really sweet of her. Oh, and William and Maxine are making our wedding invitations."

"A successful morning for both of us then," said Paul before kneeling and talking to Nikki's stomach. "Hello in there, it's Daddy here, I can't wait to meet you."

Nikki burst into tears and a concerned Paul immediately leapt up to comfort her. "Hey, what's wrong?" he asked.

Nikki grabbed a tissue and wiped her eyes. "Oh, probably just pregnancy hormones, I never thought we'd ever be talking about a baby. I'm so happy."

"It's killing me not being able to tell anyone," said Paul.

"I know, But it's only for a few more weeks." She had been booked in for her first scan two weeks after Christmas.

Once Pippa and Red had returned from Manchester Nikki wandered down to the square.

"How did you get on in the dancing competition?" she asked Pippa.

"We got the silver medal. I think that we could possibly have won the gold, but I lost my footing at one point."

"Oh, what a shame. I'm sure you'll win the gold next time."

"Fingers crossed," replied Pippa. "We've won a lot of gold medals over the years; we've been incredibly lucky. You'll have to come and watch next time there's a more local competition."

"Perhaps we could hold a competition here at the folly next year when we have an open day," Nikki loved thinking of new and innovative ideas for the folly.

"That would be great fun," agreed Pippa. "Now, let's talk about wedding dresses. What do you have in mind?"

Nikki pointed to a 1950's dress with a full skirt and petticoats sitting on a mannequin. "I was thinking about something like that. Not in white as I've been married before. If you have time, would you also be able to make Daisy and Ava similar dresses as they're going to be my bridesmaids."

"I'll make the time for you," said Pippa. "I bet Mabel and Cleo will be pleased that the wedding will provide a distraction from the usual Christmas Eve excitement."

"You're probably right," replied Nikki.

Pippa walked over to her shelves filled with rolls of material. She picked one up and rolled it out on her table. "How about this?" It was a sequined rose gold lace fabric. Nikki knew at once that it would be perfect for her wedding dress. "I absolutely love it!" she exclaimed.

Pippa returned from the shelves with a full ivory coloured petticoat to go underneath the dress. "I think that this would finish the look too," she said.

"Oh, and how about this?" she added tapping on her iPad. She turned the screen round to show Nikki a white faux fur stole.

"This would keep your shoulders warm while you take your vows," Pippa said.

"I'm so glad that I came to see you," said Nikki as she leaned over to hug Pippa.

"OK, let's take some measurements then," said Pippa getting down to business.

"Um, could you give me a little bit of wiggle room on the waist measurement?" Nikki blushed. "Just in case I feel a little bloated as the evening progresses. I'd hate to have to change out of my beautiful dress," she lied.

Pippa gave Nikki a knowing smile. "Message received and understood," she replied.

After school that day, Ava, and Daisy were extremely excited to be measured for their bridesmaid's dresses and were dancing around so much that Pippa had to ask them to pretend to be statues so that she could take their measurements.

When Nikki returned home she looked very tired. "I can't believe how tiring wedding preparations are." She sighed.

Paul immediately went into protective mode. "Go and have one of your relaxing baths. Then you're doing nothing else for the rest of the day."

"I love you, Paul Archer," said Nikki, hugging Paul.

"And I love you too, soon-to-be Nikki Archer."

"Have you decided on what you're wearing on our wedding day?"

"It's all arranged," said Paul with a smile. "I think you'll be pleased."

The next week passed uneventfully. Nikki organised the catering for their wedding. She had asked the company to provide a buffet rather than a sit-down meal as she was mindful of how much people ate on Christmas day, herself included.

One evening, Paul and Nikki were binge-watching a box set of a comedy series that they both loved. Paul's phone rang. He frowned, wondering who could be calling at ten o'clock. He saw that it was Richard. He knew his parents, Chris, and all their other friends had gone into town for a Christmas meal.

"Hi, Dad, is everything OK?" he asked and then listened with a serious look on his face.

"We'll be right there." He put his arm round Nikki, who froze, knowing that it wasn't good news.

"What's happened?"

Paul sighed. "They think Chris has had a heart attack."

Nikki burst into hysterical tears. "No, not Dad. Please don't let it be true."

Paul gently pulled her up onto her feet. "Come on, let's get ourselves to the hospital. We can find out more then." Paul drove them down the country lanes towards the town, neither of them spoke. Nikki was still crying. They parked outside of the Accident and Emergency department and found Richard waiting for them outside looking grim.

"How's Dad?" cried Nikki.

"He's had a heart attack but he's responding well and he's awake," Richard replied.

They walked towards the bay where Chris was being treated and one of the nurses led them to the family room for a chat.

"Hi, I understand that you're Chris's daughter?" he asked.

"Yes, I'm Nikki," she replied, her heart pounded. She was also aware that she was shaking. Paul noticed too and gripped her hand in support.

"So, your father has had a heart attack and he'll be going down into surgery shortly. As with every surgery I just wanted to make you aware of the risks involved," said the nurse, who then went through the consent form with them.

Nikki and Paul both nodded.

"Can I go to see him now?" she asked, wiping her face with a tissue not wanting Chris to see her distress.

"Of course, you can," replied the nurse. "He's been asking to see you."

They walked along the corridor and into the bay where Chris was being treated. He looked very frail lying there with an oxygen mask on along with various wires and leads attached to monitors. His eyes were closed.

"Dad, it's me," she whispered, trying hard not to cry again.

Chris opened his eyes and turned his head to look at his daughter. "I'm sorry love, I don't want to worry you."

"Don't be daft," Nikki replied. "They're going to make you better."

"I'm having an operation tonight," said Chris, his chin wobbled. "If I don't recover please don't postpone your wedding, promise me now."

"Dad, of course you're going to get better. Don't think like that. Besides…" She turned to look at Paul who knew what she was asking him with her eyes, and he gave a slight nod. "You're going to be a grandad next summer."

Paul heard his mum give a slight gasp as she also heard the news. Both she and Richard were standing with Paul at the other end of the cubicle.

"A grandad, eh?" said Chris, and his eyes widened. "Well, I've got to recover now. I don't want to miss out on my lovely Nikki being a mum."

"Oh, Dad," was all that she could say before she started to cry again, and she could feel that his cheeks were also wet with tears.

A doctor walked into the cubicle. "Chris, we're going to take you down to the theatre now," he said before turning to Nikki. "We're going to fit your dad with a stent and then afterwards he will be taken up to the cardiac ward. It's going to be a few hours until Chris is out of surgery and in recovery. You're more than welcome to wait here, or you could go home and one of us can call you."

"Go home, love," said Chris. "You need all the rest you can get now that you're expecting. I'm so happy for you both."

They wheeled Chris's bed away down the corridor to the theatre and then Janet gave Nikki a huge hug.

"I'm so sorry about Chris, but I think your news would have given him that extra lift. Congratulations, we're incredibly happy for you both." She smiled.

"We didn't want to tell anyone until after our scan in January," said Nikki. "Would you mind if we didn't tell the rest of the family until then?"

"We understand and of course the others can wait to be told," replied Janet.

"I think I'd better phone Jess and Stuart," said Nikki not looking forward to that task.

"Let's go outside to the car and phone them from there," suggested Paul before turning to his parents.

"You might as well go home now," he said to them. "I also think that we should go home too."

"No," said Nikki firmly. "I'm not leaving him."

They walked out to the car and Nikki dialled Jessica's phone. It rang for ages before it was finally answered.

"Nikki?" Jessica asked above the noise of what sounded like a night club. "I can't hear very well, hang on. What's up?" asked Jessica sounded more irritated than concerned. They waited for a moment until it became quieter.

"Dad's had a heart attack and is in surgery at the moment," said Nikki shakily.

"Oh, so presumably the operation will fix the problem?" Jessica asked.

"They seem to think so yes, but he looked so frail lying in the hospital bed," replied Nikki.

"This couldn't have happened at a more inconvenient time," said Jessica.

"I'm sorry?" Nikki gasped. "What's so important in your life that would make Dad's heart attack seem like an inconvenience?"

"Don't talk to me like that," replied Jessica. "If you must know, Guy is busy networking now. Contacts in business are so important. Surely your fiancé would know all about that. Although—" Jess stopped speaking as if she was considering something. "Maybe it would make good sense for us to come to visit now, Paul could probably open a lot of doors for Guy."

Nikki shook her head, dumbstruck at her sister's selfish attitude.

Paul suddenly spoke, "This is Paul, Jessica. If you want to visit, then come for the right reasons. I will not be having any business meetings with your boyfriend. If he's as selfish as you seem to be, then he doesn't sound like the sort of person I would want to do business with anyway," he said, disgusted at Jessica's indifference to Chris's situation.

Jessica promptly ended the call.

"Wow, just wow!" Paul shook his head. "I know you've said that your sister is selfish, but I honestly can't believe what I've just heard. Have you ever met this Guy chap?" He could see the sadness on Nikki's face, and he leaned across and gently stroked her cheek. His family was close, he had been appalled at the indifference Nikki's brother and sister had demonstrated towards her and their dad Chris.

"Just once," Nikki replied. "They said that they were coming to visit after eighteen months without hearing from them. Dad was looking forward to it. He asked me to cook a special roast dinner and he bought some nice wine too. About half an hour into their visit Jessica asked if either of us could stump up fifty thousand pounds to put into Guy's latest business venture. When we declined, they left straight away."

"They sound like horrible people," said Paul. He couldn't ever imagine treating his parents like that.

"Oh, they really are." She had sadly come to accept the fact that Jess and Stuart would never really be part of her life. She envied the closeness that Paul had with Mike, Tom and his parents.

"Are you going to phone Stuart now?" asked Paul feeling sorry that Nikki was about to put herself through another uncomfortable phone call.

"Yep, although I'm not expecting much from him either," replied Nikki.

Stuart picked up almost straight away. "Nikki? What's up?"

"Dad's had a heart attack," said Nikki. Her chest grew tight as she remembered how frail he had looked just before he had been taken down to the operating theatre. "He's in surgery at the moment."

Stuart sniffled down the phone. "Is he going to be OK?"

"He's having a stent fitted. They think he'll recover although there are always risks with any operation," replied Nikki.

"Please keep me informed of his progress," said Stuart.

"Aren't you going to come down and visit him?" asked Nikki, her heart sinking at the thought that her other sibling was also not so bothered about their dad.

"I'm afraid not," said Stuart. "It's best that I don't."

"What's that supposed to mean?" demanded Nikki. What a feeble thing to say.

"This isn't the time for a deep and meaningful chat right now. Maybe another time. Let me know how the operation goes," he said before ending the call.

Paul shook his head. Poor Nikki, she seemed to be the only person who cared about Chris. He was such a nice person. Paul couldn't understand why Jessica and Stuart were so distant.

"So, what's Stuart's story, then?"

"He was always very introverted and spent most of his teenage years in his bedroom which he'd decorated black listening to gloomy music. He dyed his hair black and wore black makeup, too. I think the word to best describe him was an Emo," said Nikki, remembering the oppressive mood in the house at the time.

Paul nodded.

"He's also incredibly intelligent and studied the classics at university. He took some scholarly type of job up in the north of England and we haven't seen him since," said Nikki.

"I sort of got the impression that he thought that a visit wouldn't be well received by your dad," said Paul.

"I don't know why he's come to that conclusion," replied Nikki. "He's never fallen out with Dad as far as I know."

"Well, I'm more concerned about you right now. Are you sure you don't want to go home and get some sleep? We can come back first thing in the morning," said Paul worried that Nikki might make herself ill.

Nikki shook her head. "I want to be here when he comes out of recovery. Why don't you go home and get some rest?"

"No, as you've pointed out to me a few times this year, we're a team. If you want to stay then I'm here for you. And remember, there's still ten days or so before our wedding. Chris could well be home by then," said Paul.

Nikki hoped that Chris would be home in time for their wedding, it wouldn't be the same without him.

CHAPTER TWENTY-ONE

It was Christmas Eve at last. The morning frost covered all the leaves and trees in the garden with a white coating. When Nikki had gone out to feed the birds, she could see her breath and she shivered. It was bitterly cold. The water on the bird feeder was frozen solid. The forecast was for snow. As the day progressed the ominous looking clouds confirmed what everybody was hoping for, a white Christmas and this added to the excitement of the day. The children kept looking out of the windows to look for any sign of the flurries of snow. By three o'clock in the afternoon, Nikki was standing in Cleo's bedroom getting ready for her wedding. The ceremony was to take place at four.

"Your dress is stunning," said Cleo.

Pippa had certainly produced the most beautiful 1950's style wedding dress. It was made from the sequined rose gold lace material that Nikki had chosen just a few weeks before. It fell to just below Nikki's knees. The straps of the dress were made from white lace with tiny hearts sewn in. The ivory petticoats below the skirt gave a lovely, full, swishy effect. She slipped on a pair of ivory coloured kitten-heeled shoes. To top the look Nikki wore a crystal-embellished fascinator on her head. Nikki felt like a princess in her wedding outfit, she had been worried that she wouldn't look her best for the wedding. For the last few days, she had started to suffer from severe morning sickness.

Cleo applied Nikki's makeup. She had found a rose gold eyeshadow with matching lipstick and had just applied the lightest touch of bronzer to Nikki's pale face. "I bet you can't wait to jet off to Cyprus on Boxing Day to enjoy the lovely sunshine," said Cleo enviously.

"I could certainly do with the rest and relaxation," replied Nikki. "I'm really looking forward to it."

The final addition was to put on her mother Stella's pearl earrings and matching necklace. Cleo wrapped the white faux fur stole around Nikki's shoulders.

"There, all done, you look beautiful. Right, let's get the bridesmaids in." She walked out onto the landing and called downstairs, "Ava, Daisy, time to get dressed for the wedding."

Nikki smiled when the little girls screamed in excitement as they rushed up the stairs.

Mabel came up to help get them ready. "Ava, Daisy, you need to stay nice and calm now. You have an important job being Nikki's bridesmaids."

At these words the girls calmed down straight away. The girls slipped into their dresses which were almost identical to Nikki's except that theirs had puffed sleeves and no white lace. They wore stretchy rose gold hairbands on their heads and pretty pumps on their feet. They were both thrilled when they had some eyeshadow and lip gloss applied as a special treat.

"You look very pretty, girls," said Mabel, taking out her phone to join Cleo and Nikki in taking photos of them in all their finery.

Cleo looked very elegant in a baby blue coat dress with a matching pillbox hat. Mabel was dressed in a creamy yellow two-piece suit with a matching feathery fascinator.

"I wonder what the men are all wearing?" pondered Nikki.

"My lips are well and truly sealed." Cleo smiled. She had been present when a tailor had come up to her house to measure the men up for the wedding suits.

"Half an hour to go," said Mabel.

All the wedding guests were turning up at Paul and Nikki's house. Nikki, Cleo, and Connie had worked hard the day before on getting the garden looking wonderful for the wedding. Chairs had been set up all along the large patio under a gazebo with heaters supplied to keep the guests warm during the ceremony. Soon, a text arrived on Cleo's phone saying that it was time for them to go round to the house.

"This is it," she said to Nikki, who smiled back at her. "It's showtime!"

Downstairs lying on the kitchen island was Nikki's bouquet, the girl's posies and the corsages for Cleo and Mabel.

This was the first time that Nikki had seen any of the flowers, and she had to blink back the tears. Connie had surpassed herself. Her bouquet was made up of white roses with pink calla lilies and deep burgundy foliage. There were Connie's trademark crystals on sheer white ribbons woven in amongst the flowers. It was stunning. The girls held posies of white roses which matched the corsages worn by their mothers.

Nikki could hear the murmuring of voices as they walked into the house. The guests were now assembled on the patio. The trees in the garden were wrapped in bright white fairy lights. On the sides of the pathways were flickering lanterns. A huge swag of tiny, coloured fairy lights seemed to fall in waves from the fence at the far end of the garden. An enormous rose gold and white balloon arch stretched right over the width of the garden.

The wedding ceremony was to take place at the pergola which sat in the paved area that Nikki and Paul had designed halfway up the garden. Connie had wrapped it in fresh eucalyptus and winter honeysuckle. She had included some more of the sheer white ribbons covered in crystals and they glistened in the tiny white lights that had been added to complete the wonderful effect. Inside the house Connie had created a beautiful flower wall filled with fragrant yellow and white roses to provide the perfect backdrop for the wedding photos.

Paul, Mike, and Tom were waiting at the pergola. They were all wearing deep blue checked suits with matching waistcoats and crisp white shirts. They wore blue suede shoes. To finish the look, they wore bow ties which matched the shoes.

Nikki smiled as she reached the patio doors and saw Chris sitting in a wheelchair just inside. As she reached him he slowly got up out of the chair. Both he and Richard had also decided to wear the same outfits as the others. Nikki thought that her dad had never looked so handsome and dapper. The surgery had given him a new lease of life although he would have to take it easy for a while.

"I know your mother will be watching today," he whispered, and Nikki nodded.

Her favourite Ed Sheeran song filled the air, the same song that was playing when Paul had proposed to her. Holding onto to Chris's arm she walked up towards her waiting groom. Ava and Daisy walked behind Nikki giggling and smiling. Once

Chris had delivered his daughter to her husband to be, he walked back to the patio with Mike and Tom.

Paul couldn't take his eyes off his bride. "You look so beautiful, Nikki."

Summer the registrar smiled at the bride and groom, grateful for the patio heater that had been placed inside the pergola. An iPad was propped up on a specially prepared ledge giving Ruth a front-row seat for the wedding.

"Are you ready?" she asked, and Paul and Nikki nodded.

Just as she opened her book ready to start the ceremony, tiny flakes of snow fell from the sky. It was magical.

After Summer's introduction to the ceremony, Paul read aloud the vows he had written for his bride. "Nikki, I'm so happy that you've come into my life. I can't imagine a world without you in it. I promise to love you and protect you for the rest of our lives. You are my best friend as well as my partner. You have made me happy and a much better man for knowing you," he said.

It was Nikki's turn next. "Paul, the moment I met you I felt the attraction between us. I know I've met my soulmate. I promise to look after you and love you eternally," she said almost in a whisper. She didn't ever want to forget this moment.

The snowflakes were starting to settle on the garden as Paul and Nikki slipped on their identical platinum wedding bands inscribed with the date. Then, Summer declared them to be husband and wife.

"You may kiss the bride," she announced, and Paul swept Nikki into his arms and kissed her tenderly as their guests clapped and cheered.

Fireworks exploded above the house and the cascade of colours filled the sky.

"Let's get into the warm house and party!" Paul shouted out as, despite how pretty the falling snow was, it was freezing cold, and the guests were more than happy to oblige.

Tom had created a playlist for the evening and as everyone gathered inside the music filled the air including several traditional Christmas songs. Paul and Nikki walked round to speak to their guests. Nikki was thrilled to see that Amanda, Stuart and little Phoebe had been able to come after all. Phoebe had been poorly earlier on in the week. Amanda's parents Carol and Jim had also turned up and Nikki felt emotional, happy that her former in-laws were there to support her. She was thrilled to see Derek and Sue along with Matt and his fiancée Erica.

Paul was pleased to see that Anna his agent and her husband had been able to make it to the wedding. They had very kindly offered Paul and Nikki the use of their villa in Cyprus for their honeymoon. Two of his oldest friends from university Tim and Alan had also come along with their wives and children.

Nikki had never felt so happy. This wedding had felt much more personal than her marriage to Harry and she truly hoped that he was as happy as she was today.

The caterers walked round the room offering glasses of champagne for the toast. Tom tapped on his glass to get everybody's attention.

"I would like to propose a toast to the bride and groom." Everybody raised their glasses as Paul and Nikki danced to Ed Sheeran's song *Perfect*.

When everybody headed towards the buffet, Paul pulled Nikki to one side.

"Come with me," he said, leading her towards the snug where they watched tv in the evenings. On the wall was one of Nikki's paintings of the garden her mother had created. Nikki's hands went to her mouth in disbelief, she couldn't believe what she was seeing. Although she had been blown away that all her paintings at her exhibition had sold, she had felt sad about this painting going to somebody else's home. It would never mean as much to them as it did to her.

"Paul, I can't believe it. Thank you so much, this means the world to me," said Nikki full of emotion.

"I couldn't let anybody else buy paintings that meant so much to you and Chris," Paul replied. "When your dad gets home later, he will find the other painting up on his wall."

Nikki threw her arms around Paul. Chris would be so happy with his surprise gift.

"What have I done to deserve such a lovely, thoughtful husband?" said Nikki.

"Well, I happen to have a lovely, thoughtful wife too, so we're a good match," replied Paul kissing her.

Later, the music stopped, and Chris stood up to address the room. He looked nervous; he wasn't used to speaking up like this.

"Nikki, you've made me so proud today. Would you join me in dancing to the song that meant so much to me and your mum?" he asked.

Nikki walked towards him, and they danced to Etta James singing *At Last*. As the song ended everyone clapped as Nikki hugged her father tightly. "I love you, Dad," she whispered in his ear.

After their dance, the sound of jingling bells filled the room.

Mike opened the patio door and looked up into the sky. "Kids, come here!" he called out. Noah, Daisy, Ava, and Riley who was dressed in a dinosaur onesie and had been as good as gold all day, charged towards him. The other children at the wedding dashed out too.

"What is it, Daddy?" Ava jumped up and down with excitement.

"Look up there," instructed Mike as several of the other wedding guests spilled out onto the patio.

Father Christmas was riding across the sky in his sleigh being pulled along by his reindeer. He waved to the children below and a deep *"Merry Christmas everybody"* boomed around them.

The children and most of the adults were captivated by the scene.

"Santa! Santa!" cried the children in excitement hardly believing what they were seeing.

"How on earth did you manage that?" asked Amanda looking impressed.

"One of Tom's friends works in the entertainment industry, particularly with holograms and he called in a favour," replied Richard.

"How magical for the children," replied Amanda. "Isn't technology wonderful."

When the image disappeared from the sky the children were all full of excitement, even eight-year-old Noah who had been starting to wonder if Father Christmas was real.

A little while later, Mike carrying a sleeping Riley and Cleo holding a very tired Ava's hand found Paul and Nikki.

"This has been a wonderful day," said Cleo. "I'll never forget it."

"I saw Santa," said Ava, her eyelids droopy.

Nikki hugged her friend. "Thank you so much for everything Cleo," she said. "I'm glad we've become such close friends."

"Me too," said Cleo, wiping an uncharacteristic tear away. "Enjoy your time in Cyprus both of you."

Once all the guests and the caterers had left, Paul and Nikki sat quietly looking out at the beautiful garden now covered in snow.

"Happy?" asked Paul.

"So happy," Nikki said with a sigh.

"We don't have to tidy anything up," said Paul. "We're at Mum and Dad's tomorrow and then Cleo has promised that everything will be spick and span by the time we return from our honeymoon."

Nikki slipped off her shoes and rubbed her feet. "I wouldn't have the energy to tidy up even if I wanted to," she replied.

"Wasn't it wonderful to see the children so excited to see Father Christmas." Nikki had also been impressed by the special effect.

"Mind you, the children will be expecting to see him every year now," she said.

Paul laughed. "That thought crossed my mind too," he said.

"What a year it's been," said Nikki. "When I came to start work here at the folly I never thought that by Christmas I would be married with a baby on the way."

"We've got so much to look forward to next year," said Paul as he kissed his new wife. "The best is yet to come."

THE END

ALSO BY E.H. STEPHENSON

Archer's Folly Book 2 – Secrets, shocks, and surprises

Welcome back to Archer's Folly!

Life is looking pretty good for Paul and Nikki Archer. They're looking forward to becoming parents and the folly has successfully opened. Now they are thinking up new and exciting ways to expand.

When Nikki gets some surprising news about the painting she found in her father's loft, it isn't too long before her estranged sister, Jessica, turns up and decides to stay.

Paul's brother, Tom, has been attracted to Heather McBain ever since she moved into one of the units in the Artisan Square where she works making intricate silver jewellery. But although Heather enjoys Tom's company, she is determined never to get involved with anybody again. When Tom finds out why he realises that it will take more than charm and good looks to gain her trust.

Red and Pippa also live in the Artisan square and have been happily married for fifteen years. But, when an unexpected visitor arrives it leaves their relationship hanging on a thread.

ABOUT THE AUTHOR

I grew up in Brighton and from a very early age I always enjoyed writing stories. I used to write little plays in junior school.

It was always a dream to become a published author. A year ago, I suddenly got the idea for Archer's Folly, a contemporary romance and I quickly fell in love with the characters in the story. I have loads of ideas for future books in the Archer's Folly series and I'm really looking forward to developing the plots and characters for you.

Now I live in Hertfordshire with my husband, Mark. I have two grown up sons.

Printed in Great Britain
by Amazon